Top Deck Twenty!
Best West Coast Sea Stories!

Cover Photo: Crewman aboard thirty-six-foot Coast Guard motor lifeboat prepares to heave line to stranded fifty-foot yacht *Enid III* in Depoe Bay channel entrance. (Photo by author)

Top Deck Twenty!
Best West Coast Sea Stories!

Stan Allyn

Binford & Mort Publishing
Portland, Oregon

Printed in the United States of America

Library of Congress Catalog Card Number: 89-60951

ISBN: 0-8323-0469-7

First Edition 1989
Second Edition 1990

Dedicated to Cheryl Buehler who kept me
at it until the book was finished.

FOREWORD
by Senator Mark O. Hatfield

During my childhood in Dallas, Oregon, the family trip to the coast was an annual highlight. There never seemed to be a limit to the places I could explore and the things I could find, whether it was the pieces of glass brought onto the beach from some faraway land with each new high tide or the cities and towns along the 400 miles of coastline. As I gazed out over the water and into the horizon, that vast expanse always made me feel even smaller than I actually was.

A great many years have passed since those family trips, but my love for the Pacific coast, her secrets and her stories, has never changed. Instead of going with my parents, however, I now go with my children and with their children, passing on to them the mysteries and wonders of the coast.

In *Top Deck Twenty!*, Captain Stan Allyn has documented some of those secrets and stories, some of those mysteries and wonders. Whether it's the amazing tale of that durable dredge *Pacific* or the story of a hunt for grey whales, Captain Allyn treats his stories with the reverence of someone who belongs as much to the sea as he does to the land.

Of course there is history to be found in these pages. For those who wonder how Cannon Beach was named, the answer is here. So too is the answer for those who wonder about the fate of the USS *Milwaukee* or the Steam Schooner *Brooklyn*.

But what is really in these pages is a celebration, of the Pacific Coast and those ships and men who have shared in her majesty. The invitation to join the celebration exists on the craggy rocks, the sandy beaches, the old ships and, most of all, in the imagination of anybody who has ever stood and gazed at the vast expanse.

Contents

1. "Stretch Out on That Deck or I'll Blast Your Head Off!"

"Stretch out on that deck or I'll blast your head off!"

The deadly command triggered a piracy attempt aboard a 20th-century, wireless-equipped passenger steamship off the Oregon coast so fantastic it makes the exploits of Spanish-main pirates appear as tea parties by comparison.

The bizarre affair was hatched in the mind of a 30-year-old sailor named French West at San Francisco in 1909.

West, who had served several years in the Merchant Marine, where he held a second mate's license, quit that service in 1909 and enlisted in the Navy. He was assigned to the USS *Pensacola*, a training ship stationed at Yerba Buena island in San Francisco Bay.

While aboard the *Pensacola*, he struck up an acquaintance with George Washington Wise, 26, of Boston. After cautiously sounding Wise out, to insure against betrayal, he unfolded his piratical plan.

During his Merchant Marine service West had learned that fortunes in Alaskan gold were frequently carried aboard ships plying the Alaska trade, bound for the mint at San Francisco. They'd desert from the Navy, he explained, head for Seattle and take passage on a Frisco-bound gold ship. When the ship arrived off the Oregon coast, they'd hold up the crew, commandeer the ship, run it ashore and make off with the gold.

A few days later they deserted the *Pensacola* and took the steamer *Beaver* to Seattle, where they lost no time rounding up the tools of their trade: A double-barreled shotgun, a revolver, and a length of line which they cut into 50 short lengths with which to tie up the crew.

S. S. Buckman (From author's collection)

Then they cased the waterfront and soon discovered that the Alaska-Pacific Navigation company's steamer *Buckman,* which was later rechristened *Admiral Evans* when it sailed under the burgee of the famous Admiral line, was in port loading for San Francisco. West knew that it regularly carried gold, along with passengers and general cargo.

They purchased two steerage tickets for passage to San Francisco and on August 19, 1910, their guns and line hidden in their gear, boarded the ship.

The *Buckman* sailed shortly after they were aboard, clearing Elliot bay and Juan de Fuca strait, and standing southward down the coast for San Francisco.

The pirates remained to themselves through the first hours at sea, quietly sizing up the ship for the best means of attack.

Shortly after midnight, August 21, West outlined the plan to Wise. He knew that the ship was about 20 miles off the Oregon coast in the vicinity of the Umpqua River mouth.

Stealthily they cat-footed their way to the dimly-lighted wheelhouse and stepped inside.

Second Mate Fred Plath and Quartermaster Otto Kocklmeister at the helm, looked up in alarm as the two silently entered. To temporarily allay their suspicions, West said they'd come to ask the mate to search the ship for a watch he'd lost.

While Plath was contemplating this, West, nodding to Wise, whipped out his shotgun, leveled it at the mate's head, and ordered him to stretch out on the deck or be blasted.

Staring into the shotgun's yawning muzzle in shocked disbelief, Plath sank to the deck, while Kocklmeister, the barrel of Wise's revolver pressed to the back of his head, stood at the wheel cursing vigorously.

"Where's the captain?" demanded West.

"In his cabin," growled Plath.

"Keep these two covered," he barked at Wise. "I'm going to take care of the captain. If they make a move, let 'em have it!"

Keeping the shotgun pointed into the wheelhouse, he backed out the starboard door, then bolted down the ladder to the deck below, raced aft to the captain's cabin and burst inside.

Captain Edwin B. Wood, startled from his sleep, was attempting to reach for his revolver when West fired both barrels directly at him, killing him instantly.

Alarmed by the shots, Wise stepped from the wheelhouse to see what had happened. As he did so Kocklmeister reached overhead and yanked the whistle cord.

The shrieks of the whistle blasted the night apart as West bolted from the captain's cabin and rushed to the bridge, reloading as he ran.

"Who blew that whistle?" he demanded profanely.

"That rat there!" answered Wise, waving his revolver toward Kocklmeister.

Swearing profusely, West thrust his shotgun in Kocklmeister's face, but before he could fire, the sound of running feet came to him on the port side of the wheelhouse. He spun around just in time to cover Chief Mate Richard C. Brennan, who'd been jarred awake by the shotgun and whistle blasts and was rushing to investigate.

West ordered him to hoist his hands and stand against

the port bridge rail. Then he ordered Plath to get up and stand alongside Brennan.

Seconds later Chief Engineer John Califass, followed by a number of crewmen, rushed up the darkened port companionway to the bridge deck.

Confronted by the pirates' guns, they halted in their tracks and one by one were lined up against the rail, their hands above their heads. The pirates now had two thirds of the ship's crew under their guns.

"Go smash the wireless!" West ordered Wise.

But Wise's nerve had broken. Instead of obeying he rushed below decks and hid. When he failed to return West swore to the crew that he'd kill every last one of them and take the ship single handed.

His attention was momentarily diverted when a crewman approached the bridge on the opposite side of the wheelhouse. That moment was all Engineer Callfass needed. He leaped from the bridge deck through a skylight shaft above the wheelhouse, crashing into the galley below.

In the resulting confusion the officers and men scattered in all directions, plunging down ladders and leaping over rails.

Screaming vituperatively that he'd blow them all to hell, West climbed to the top of the wheelhouse from where he could shoot anyone attempting to approach the bridge.

During the scramble, Chief Mate Brennan had succeeded in bolting to the captain's cabin. He snatched up the dead captain's revolver and inched his way to the bridge ladder.

Concealed by the protective darkness, he crawled slowly up the ladder and at last slipped into the wheelhouse undetected. Motioning Kocklmeister to silence, he stood in a corner of the wheelhouse waiting for West to come down.

After a seemingly endless wait, he heard West moving across the deck above. Seconds later the pirate appeared at the port wheelhouse door.

"Drop that gun and hold up your hands!" roared Brennan.

Instead of complying the pirate whipped up the shotgun and blasted a wild shot into the wheelhouse, shattering the wheel but missing Brennan and Kocklmeister.

Instantly Brennan opened up a fusillade on the pirate, who returned the fire with a second blast from the shotgun. The shot came closer but again missed the two men.

Abruptly the pirate bolted out the door, plunged down the ladder, raced aft along the deck, hurled himself over the side into the sea and sank from sight.

Brennan quickly organized a stem-to-stern search for Wise, who was found in his bunk, whimpering hysterically. He surrendered without resistance and was clapped into irons.

Brennan hurried to the bridge and relieved Kocklmeister, who had remained at the damaged but usable helm through the entire affray.

The following day the *Buckman,* under Brennan's command, steamed into San Francisco bay. It was met by a police launch, which came alongside while a squad of officers climbed aboard and placed Wise under arrest.

Later he was arraigned in the United States circuit court at San Francisco on a charge of murder on the high seas, for which the death penalty is mandatory. But the case never came to trial, for on November 4, 1910, George Washington Wise was adjudged insane and placed in a mental institution.

Officers and crewmen all agreed that had Wise not lost his nerve and fled, the pirates might have succeeded in their fantastic plan to commandeer the ship.

But even if they had, the irony of fate would have spelled failure in the end, for on this of all voyages the S.S. *Buckman* carried no gold.

Brennan subsequently had a notable career. In World War I he commanded the S.S. *Yale,* which carried 286,000 soldiers, nurses, prisoners and wounded without a casualty. In World War II he commanded the liberty ship *Nathaniel Hawthorne* and went down with his ship when it was torpedoed off Trinidad, November 4, 1942.

Captain R.C. Brennan went down with his ship, torpedoed on November 4, 1942. (From author's collection)

2. How Peacock Spit Was Named

Sister ship to the *Peacock* (From author's collection)

The spanking new 559-ton U.S. Sloop of War *Peacock*, twenty-two guns and 140 crew, commanded by Lt. William Hudson, dropped anchor in Oahu, Sandwich Islands, (now

Hawaiian), after exploring the South Pacific for many months in 1841.

In Oahu, Lieutenant Hudson received orders from Lt. Charles Wilkes directing him to proceed northwest to the Oregon Territory and there to chart the capricious Columbia River entrance.

While in port at Oahu, Lieutenant Hudson met Captain Spaulding, master of the *Lausanne*, who was fresh from Fort George (Astoria) and a veteran of many crossings of the Columbia River bar. He furnished Lieutenant Hudson with written directions of entry into the Columbia.

The *Peacock* arrived off the bar the morning of July 17, 1841, enveloped in cotton-wool fog and no wind, which forced the ship to heave to.

The following day a light breeze cleared the fog and filled the *Peacock's* sails, and Hudson, stationing himself on the ships fo'c's'l with Spaulding's written instructions, and placing one of the officers high in the foresail top-yard to watch for shoals, he ordered all hands to work the ship into the river.

Presently crashing breakers dead ahead, (normal at that spot), shot terror into the *Peacock's* men, and mistakenly assuming his course to be too far south, Hudson ordered the helm hard to port to clear the white water.

The maneuver worked the *Peacock* out of the channel, and she struck!

The young captain shouted for helm alee to bring the ship into the wind and haul off. She struck again!

Hudson's frantic shouts ordered the sails furled and the anchor dropped!

Lt. George Emmons launched the ship's cutter and shoved off from the pounding ship to sound the area.

A shrieking northwest wind began blasting the area with black clouds spawning driving rain, which shrouded the ship and added to the hell's broth whipped up by an increasingly strong ebb tide in head-on collision with incoming seas.

Emmons and his boat crew were barely able to fight their way back to the precarious safety of the embattled ship.

Each cresting sea heaved the ship high, then slammed

her back on the concrete-hard sand!

Slashing seas swept the decks and forced the pump crews to abandon their stations! The water rose alarmingly in the hull!

A wall of water tore away the rudder's iron-strapped tiller, causing the freed rudder to bang back and forth viciously against the weakened stern.

Forty-five fathoms of anchor chain holding the bow into the onslaught eased the buffeting somewhat.

The sudden cannon-like snapping of the chain spelled the end!

The crew let go another anchor, but it served only to prolong the ship's agony!

"We have no hope, but of saving the crew," wrote the Midshipman Alonzo Davis in a terse log entry.

The hell's broth sea calmed slightly about 7:00 A.M. and Hudson ordered all important ship's papers gathered up and all aboard to abandon ship with only the clothes on their backs and the important ship's papers.

Marines took their muskets and shot pouches.

The *Peacock* lay only 1½ miles from shore, but the ship's boats were forced to fight their way four miles to a safe landing spot.

The following morning Lieutenant Hudson returned to the wreck, but only the tip of the *Peacock's* bowsprit remained visible, reaching forlornly from the breaker bashed sandy tomb of the valiant vessel that endures in memory in the turbulent shoal carrying its name — Peacock Spit.

3. How Cannon Beach Was Named

The 300-ton U.S. Naval Survey schooner *Shark*, Captain Schenk commanding, was detached from the fleet at Honolulu by Commodore Sloat in the summer of 1846 and ordered to proceed northwest to survey the rivers and harbors of the Oregon Territory.

Fate decreed that shipwreck was to make her unwittingly responsible for naming a town and helping in the building of a ship that staved off starvation in another settlement.

The *Shark* arrived off the Columbia River after a twenty-five day passage, and while feeling her way across the Columbia Bar, which was mercifully calm, she met up with a lone Negro in a canoe who eased alongside, said he was a survivor of the U.S. Sloop of War, *Peacock*, wrecked at the river mouth five years earlier, and offered to pilot the ship to Fort George (Astoria).

Captain Schenk was dubious, but inasmuch as his charts were woefully vague, he put the man to work. Within an hour he rammed the ship aground on a sand bar!

After a lot of tough work with sails, rudder, and hand-heaved windlass musceling in line secured to strategically placed anchors, the *Shark* was finally hauled free.

Not wanting to risk his ship further with the erstwhile Negro pilot, whose profession proved to be ship's cook, Captain Schenk hove to, ordered him off the quarterdeck, and sent word in for a more competent pilot.

John Lettie, a pioneer, was the only qualified man available, and he piloted the schooner in to Fort George with no strain.

Her arrival was met with mixed emotions.

Fears gripped the local populous that the ship had been·sent as a war precaution in the face of imagined friction between Great Britain and the United States over the boundary question.

It was erroneously thought that the *Shark* stood ready for battle and that her survey mission was a mere cover-up.

The *Shark's* officers and British subjects at Fort George did their best to allay anxiety.

Then more trouble ensued. The *Shark's* crew worn down from long months at sea, began deserting in alarming numbers, and replacements were not to be had.

To prevent further desertions, the survey of the river mouth was hastily conducted, and the *Shark* was made ready for her final departure on September 10, 1846.

In his haste to depart, Captain Schenk made a fatal error! He did not wait for favorable sea conditions and slack flood tide, but went blundering onto this treacherous bar without checking conditions.

The *Shark* struck on the south side shoals (Jetty Sands) and was immediately slammed by vicious breakers!

In order to lighten the ship Captain Schenk ordered the cannons and all moveable objects jettisoned, and still the ship would not float free.

Within a few hours the *Shark* started breaking up and reluctantly the captain gave the order to abandon ship.

The ship's boats were launched, and the crew fought safely across the bar and to the safety of Fort George.

At the Columbia River Maritime Museum in Astoria is a boulder known as *Shark Rock* on which the survivors of the wreck inscribed the date of her loss shortly after they made landfall at Fort George.

Eighteen years later the seven survivors of the wrecked ship *Industry* made landfall in their ship's boat at Shark Rock and inscribed their own tragic story of the loss of the *Industry* March 16, 1865, with the loss of seventeen lives.

During a sewer excavation project recently, astounded workmen unearthed the rock in the vicinity of Fourteenth and Exchange Streets.

At an unknown date, after the wrecking of the *Shark*,

In 1846 the boulder stood on the shore line near the present intersection of 14th and Exchange Streets. Eighteen years later the survivors of the American Barque *Industry* inscribed the particulars of their own shipwreck on the same rock. (Photo courtesy of Don Marshall)

"Workmen unearthed Shark Rock during sewer excavations." Don Marshall

Cannon & windlass off wrecked U.S. Naval Survey Schooner *Shark*. Cannon Beach was named after this cannon. The cannon and windlass are now located at the Clatsop County Historical Society Heritage Center, Astoria, Oregon. (Photo by author)

Morning Star II under construction by citizens of Tillamook under direction of shipwright Clarence Sessions in 1959. (Photo courtesy Tillamook Pioneer Museum)

John Gerritse, one of the early settlers, spotted a cannon and windlass still attached to a portion of wreckage from the *Shark* that had drifted ashore near Arch Cape.

He hauled them ashore and set them in concrete at the Rudolf Kissling place at Hug Point, where they remained until they were moved to the east side of Highway 101 where they would be more visible and where they remain until this day.

In 1910 a post office called *Ecola* was established at a place call Elk Creek. The name of that post office was changed to *Cannon Beach* in 1922.

In 1953 two cannons were cast to resemble the original and were placed at each entrance to the community, and in 1955 Cannon Beach was incorporated as a city.

Eight years following the wrecking of the *Shark*, pioneer settlers in Tillamook, isolated by rugged mountains on the east and a dangerous bar on the west, become impoverished because of being deprived of the prosperity that trade with Portland and other valley cities would bring.

At a meeting born of desperation on September 24, 1854, the settlers decided to build their own trading ship.

Morning Star II underway from Tillamook to Portland for centennial celebration in 1959. (Photo courtesy Tillamook Pioneer Museum)

Using the mud flats as a drawing board, they planned a two-masted schooner of thirty tons and went right to work.

But it soon became apparent that there was no iron, steel or copper for bolts and fittings.

The Indians told them of considerable metal on the wreck of the *Shark* at the mouth of the Columbia, and with pack horses they made the tough trek over Neahkahnie Mountain to the site and procured enough metal to return to Tillamook, set up a blacksmith shop and hammer out all their needing fittings.

On January 1, 1855, the first vessel built in Tillamook County slid down a balky ways, greased with tallow rendered from a slaughtered steer.

Hailed as "the blessing of a new Tillamook County", she was christened the *Morning Star* and soon provided the beleagured settlers with a lusty trade in dairy products, sugar, coffee, flour, tools, cloth and numerous vital necessities.

A replica of the *Morning Star* is on display on the grounds of the Tillamook County Creamery Association.

In her the U.S. Naval Survey schooner *Shark* lives on in spirit.

4. The Durable Dredge *Pacific*

One of the toughest ships ever to sail Pacific Coast waters is the homely little 180-foot Army Corps of Engineers seagoing hopper dredge *Pacific*, home-ported at Portland, Oregon.

For over 50 years since it was built by the Bethlehem Shipbuilding Co. in San Francisco in 1937, the *Pacific* has been challenging Pacific Coast rivers, harbors, channels and rough bars from Grays Harbor, Washington, to San Francisco to help keep them dredged to safe operating depths.

And it is an overseas World War II veteran.

Following the outbreak of World War II, a holler for help was shouted by armed forces officers, who cried the urgent need to deepen embattled channels and lagoons of Pacific atolls and islands to make them navigable for U.S. ships as they stormed toward Japanese homeland islands.

The *Pacific* was rapidly readied for the assignment, and early in 1943, with its complement of 44 civilian officers and crewmen, the little ship's twin 800-horsepower Fairbanks-Morse diesels churned it from its Pacific Northwest Home waters southwestward across the Pacific to Canton island, first stopping place on the air-ferry lane from the Hawaiian Islands to Australia.

Five-knot tidal currents in Canton Island's narrow entrance channel wrenched off dredging gear and continually threatened to sweep the ship against precipitous coral banks, but it did the job; then steamed to Funafuti Island in the Ellice group, northeast of Australia, and tackled tough coral that had to be blasted apart with 322 tons of high explosives before it could be dredged.

December 1947 RH-46 Portland District, Corps of Engineer Seagoing Hopper Dredge *Pacific*. Direct Drive 800 H.P., twin screw, length O.A. 180'3", beam 38'0", draft light forward 5'10", draft light aft 8'9", steel hull, hopper capacity 500 cubic yards. (From author's collection)

The tricky job completed, the *Pacific* steamed to Honolulu harbor and dredged nearly a million cubic yards of coral and sand from a rear channel entrance to safeguard the port from being blocked by the enemy.

In June, 1944, the *Pacific* roamed home to the Pacific Northwest, where instead of heaving to for a well-earned rest, it dredged West Coast waterways until February, 1945, when it again slugged southwestward to muscle tough lava sand from channels and anchorages at Iwo Jima.

This finished, the hard-pressed *Pacific* responded to the howls for dredging help bellowed by armed forces commanders at invasion-wracked Okinawa.

This writer, a Portland native familiar with the *Pacific's* dredging operations in the Pacific Northwest and a deck officer aboard a Coast Guard vessel at the invasion of Okinawa, thought he'd blown his hatches from battle fatigue when during a brief lull between around-the-clock kamikaze attacks by Japanese suicide planes he gaped at the battle-gray *Pacific* ghosting into smoke-screen-blotched Nagagusuki Wan, Okinawa's embattled main harbor (later

U.S. Engineer Dredge *Pacific* (From author's collection)

named Buckner Bay after Tenth Army General Simon Bolivar Buckner was killed in action at Okinawa).

Shells, rockets, bombs and Japanese kamikaze planes were screaming and exploding all over the place; yet the indomitable little *Pacific* clawed to her assigned dredging area and went to work.

Violent conditions under which the *Pacific* worked are poignantly illustrated by excerpts from this writer's 1945 Okinawa war diary:

3 May. Kamikaze attack. Estimate 300 planes . . . three destroyers sunk . . . 19 killed, 39 wounded, 20 missing on destroyer *Aaron Ward* . . . 35 killed, 91 wounded on light cruiser *Birmingham*.

18 May. Kamikaze attack. Twin-engine bomber flew low over us . . . Barely cleared masthead . . . bombed LST 808 500 feet on our port beam . . . blast lit sky with red flame . . . showered red hot metal chunks on our decks . . . men cry for help . . . total loss.

24 May. Kamikaze attack. Fifty raids . . . 200 planes.

25 May. Kamikaze attack. Plane crashed USS *Spectacle* . . . three killed, 11 wounded, 14 missing . . . USS *J. William Ditter* jumped by five kamikazes . . . splashed three . . . crashed by two . . . 10 killed . . . 27 wounded.

28 May. Kamikaze attack. Float plane crashed into bridge of Liberty ship SS *Livermore,* 1,000 yards on our

port beam . . . all officers killed but chief mate, who was ashore.

29 May. Night kamikaze attack. Plane followed fire trail of 40mm shells being fired from stern of destroyer . . . crashed stern . . . 40mm magazine exploded . . . 35 killed.

U.S. casualties at Okinawa totaled 49,000 men, including 12,500 dead or missing. The navy lost 36 ships and 790 planes. Japanese plane losses totaled an estimated 7,830.

Through these nightmarish conditions the doughty *Pacific* dredged doggedly on without casualty.

On October 9, 1945, her luck ran out.

On that date the worst typhoon in 20 years sledge-hammered dead center into Okinawa.

Screaming winds peaking at 186 miles per hour when the last anemometer blew out sent towering combers charging over the ocean's tormented surface and across Okinawa's bays and anchorages. The wind peaked at over 200 miles per hour, according to estimates.

The slashing wind tore the tops off the combers and shot seawater through the air like buckshot. It tore the clothes clean off an exposed man, cut his skin bleeding raw.

In the wheelhouse of our ship a man had to cup his hands around the ear of a man next to him and shout with full lung power to make himself heard above the screeching roar.

With engines pounding at ahead emergency and maximum scope of straining taut anchor chain out, our ship barely battled and held against the cataclysmic onslaught.

The radio was a cacaphonious hash of distress messages and calls for help.

The hammering wind wrought havoc, sinking, capsizing and driving ships ashore on all sides.

Some men struggled ashore from foundered ships, only to be felled by chunks of coral and debris hurtling through the air like shrapnel.

Three hundred vessels were lost or damaged during the Great Typhoon, 157 of them at Buckner Bay.

U.S. Engineer Dredge *Pacific,* damaged in typhoon at Okinawa on October 9 and 10, 1945. (From author's collection)

The plucky *Pacific* was holding its own under maximum power and maximum anchor chain scope, but at the height of the typhoon a Liberty ship to windward of it was torn from its anchorage, smashed into the straining *Pacific* and both ships were driven ashore.

After the typhoon had blown out, we passed close to the *Pacific* in our ship's launch. Seeing it smashed and listing hard aground, we figured it a total loss and foresaw its bones rusting to eternity along with scores of other wrecked ships at Okinawa.

We underestimated the tough little ship and its plucky crew.

They rounded up all the salvage equipment and help they could muster, hauled her off the beach, and she was towed to the mainland for extensive repairs.

Through the succeeding years she has steadfastly dredged West Coast waterways.

When Mount St. Helens blew May 18, 1980, it sent a massive flood of ash, silt, logs, trees, and other debris surging down the Toutle River which dumped the incredible mass into the Cowlitz River which finally disgorged it into the Columbia River.

Alarmed officials noted that the normally 40 ft. deep main ship channel shoaled to a mere 15 ft. depth virtually blocking all deep water shipping to all ports upriver from Longview, including Vancouver, Washington and Portland, Oregon.

An emergency plea for help was shouted to the Army Corps of Engineers, and again the plucky dredge *Pacific* pumped its way to hero status when with other units and equipment it dredged the channel to project depth, and prevented disaster to upriver ports.

At this writing, the *Pacific* is on a 'standby' status at the Corps of Engineers' moorage in Portland, according to Leroy Johnson of the Corps' public information office in Portland.

5. Death Held the Stakes

Death held the stakes when the three-masted British clipper ship *Atalanta* departed from Tacoma on November 14, 1898.

The voyage was to end in the worst marine disaster in the annals of seafaring on the central Oregon coast, claiming the lives of the captain and 23 of the ill-fated ship's 27-man crew.

Before sailing with a $65,000 cargo of wheat, Captain Charles McBride, skipper of the trim, white-hulled square rigger, had wagered the captains of two other sailing ships loading at Tacoma that his ship would be first to arrive at the African port all three were bound for.

The competing ships got underway several days ahead of the *Atalanta,* and to overcome this handicap Captain McBride, who had a reputation as a competent navigator and master, decided to hold a close-inshore course on the long haul southward along the Pacific Northwest coast.

This, he reasoned, would lop off many miles that would have to be traversed on the normal offshore sea route, and as his graceful, deeply-laden ship was towed by a coal-burning, smoke-belching tug across Puget Sound toward Juan de Fuca Strait, he laid out courses allowing for the barest margin of safety along the rugged, reef-ribbed Washington and Oregon coasts.

Off Cape Flattery sailors swarmed up the shrouds and stood ready at the yards, halyards and braces. A whistle blast from the tug signalled crewmen to drop the towline. The whistle unknowingly shrieked the prelude of doom.

Rapidly the unfurled sails blossomed from stem to stern and were braced for a southerly heading on a freshening

Clipper ship *Atalanta* (From author's collection)

wind. Overhead, mare's tails streaked their warning of approaching high winds and foul weather.

Visibility remained good as the big clipper beat southward along the Washington coast, enabling Captain McBride and his officers to take visual bearings on the newly-stationed lightship off Umatilla Reef, Destruction Island and other capes and promontories; thus they were able to skirt the coastline closely and save precious miles.

Off the Columbia River conditions began deteriorating with rain driving in on increasing winds, squeezing visibility down to a scant half mile. Visual bearings were no longer possible.

Still Captain McBride held to his "hedge-hopping" course. Heeling and plunging, the clipper ate up the miles.

On the black, rain-wracked night of November 16, dead reckoning placed the ship in the vicinity of Yaquina Head, but the powerful beam of the lighthouse there was blotted out by the murk.

The Atalanta plunged on. She had but a few hours to live.

Some time during the storm-lashed early morning hours of November 17 the straining clipper crunched onto a submerged reef, 17 miles south of the Alsea Bay entrance and 1½ miles offshore.

Most of the off-watch men were in their bunks. They fought their way to the lurching deck and stared horrified at a devastating scene of utter chaos.

Frantic shouts could barely be heard above a frightful din of smashing breakers, falling rigging and splintering timbers.

Hurtling seas repeatedly lifted the pounding ship, then hurled it back onto the reef's jagged jaws. Finally a massive comber smashed it down with a terrific impact that wrenched the hull in two amidships.

Men, gear and all lifeboats were swept overboard into the maelstrom.

Struggling for his life, a seaman named George Fraser, from Philadelphia, managed to drag himself into a swamped lifeboat. Then he hauled aboard John Webber, of Tarrytown, New York, who was clinging to the lifeboat's other side. The two bruised, half-frozen sailors succeeded in pulling Francis McMahon, of Belfast, Ireland, into the wallowing boat.

Around them they could hear cries for help from other crewmen, but without oars they were helpless in their efforts to reach them.

Miraculously, the floundering lifeboat was later swept onto the beach, several miles to the south, with the three sailors still clinging to it. They were the sole survivors.

Mrs. Larry (Marge) Kauffman, Waldport, granddaughter of widowed Mrs. Mary Kindred, who with her brother, John Thomas, were homesteaders in the Big Creek area at the time of the wreck, keenly recalls events that followed as related by her forbears.

"The three shipwrecked crewmen struggled ashore through the darkness," she recounted, "and were suddenly startled at the sight of several hogs, part of my grandmother's and uncle's herd.

"Mistaking them for wild animals and assuming this to be wild uninhabited country, they scrambled into some nearby pine trees, where they shivered the night out — two stark naked and the third wearing only his underwear.

"When daylight finally penetrated the murk, they

Site where *Atalanta* was wrecked off Big Creek in South Lincoln County. (Photo by author)

spotted the homestead about two miles away, and the underwear-clad sailor made his way to the house and reported the shipwreck to my astounded forbears.

"The menfolk grabbed blankets and clothing for the survivors and rushed to the beach where the lifeboat had come in.

"They found no more survivors but pulled ashore two bodies which they spotted in the surf along with all manner of wreckage and debris.

"My uncles, Jim and Lee Kindred, later buried the two dead sailors on a sandy knoll nearby.

"The whole family pitched in to take care of the castaways until they were well enough to journey to Portland for transportation to their homes."

Mrs. Chester (Marjorie) Hays, Yachats, niece of Charles Bobell, another homesteader in the Big Creek area, also has poignant memories of the shipwreck as described to her by her uncle.

"Uncle Charles described it this way," she said: "We walked three miles through the storm to the scene of the wreck. It was foggy and rainy. At first you could see the masts. I waded out to one fellow in a life preserver but could not reach him; although I talked to him.

"When he finally came ashore he was exhausted and dying. He was later buried on a nearby sandhill beside another drowned sailor."

Graves of the two sailors, surrounded by a white picket fence and marked by a ship's steering wheel and a plank from the *Atalanta* bearing its name, remained on the sandhill until they were washed away by the Good Friday tidal wave of March 27, 1964.

In the end, the sea claimed the sailors it had reached for over six decades earlier.

6. Death of a Town

The millionaire developer went violently insane during the night and was never seen again!

Mrs. T.B. Potter, wife of the dynamic founder and developer of the resort town of Bayocean on the northern Oregon coast, sobbed to neighbors the horror of her husband's rampaging through their Bayocean home in a raving fit and fleeing berserk into the murky darkness to disappear forever.

His death boded doom for the sizeable and promising town he had founded in 1907 on a four-mile-long wooded peninsula separating Tillamook Bay from the Pacific Ocean. Insidious forces began ravaging Bayocean with mounting violence and finally tore the guts out of it.

The seeds of the catastrophe — miniscule grains of sand — were sewn during the millenniums past.

Ocean-spawned rains falling on the Coast Range Mountains in western Oregon sent rivulets cascading down their westerly slopes to grow into five sizeable rivers — the Trask, Tillamook, Kilchis, Wilson and Miami.

The tools of erosion — wind, rain, frost and rushing water — slowly disintegrated ages-old rock, and tons of sediment and sand were swept seaward in the roiling rivers, which joined forces a few miles from the Pacific to carve out a great bay named Tillamook, meaning 'land of many waters' in the native Indian tongue.

During every ebb the sediment-laden waters brawled to Tillamook Bay's outlet channel where they crashed and churned in violent head-on collision with the inrushing Pacific breakers.

In the cataclysmic process hundreds of thousands of

tons of sand were tumbled, sifted and shifted between the bay and the Pacific, and through the centuries gradually built up into a low, narrow sandspit.

Borne to the spit by wind, waves and birds, grass seeds gradually took root and stabilized the sand. Plants, bushes and small trees followed, and as the centuries plodded on, nature's fantastic forces built the once-precarious spit into a respectable peninsula.

From its southern end, attached to the mainland at Cape Mears, it stretched northward four miles, where the Tillamook outlet channel funnels into the sea.

At the turn of the century it boasted a maximum height of 140 feet above sea level for over three miles of its length and was covered with lush coastal vegetation and a healthy forest of great conifers, habitat of deer, bear and smaller game.

A long level beach, prolific with razor clam beds, bordered its westerly side, and bay clams were abundant under the placid Tillamook Bay waters lapping its easterly shore. Salt water fish abounded in all the surrounding waters.

This, then was the "Shangrila" explored in 1906 by T.B. Potter, head of the T.B. Potter Realty Co., who had made a fortune in Kansas as a real estate promoter.

Traveling from Kansas to the Pacific Northwest on a vacation trip that year, Potter arrived in Portland, Oregon, inquired as to a good recreational area, and was advised to go to Tillamook, 100 miles to the west.

He made the then arduous journey to the coastal city, from where he was taken by boat to Tillamook Spit (later named Bayocean Peninsula by Potter) to try his hand at the good hunting and fishing reported there.

He was enthralled with the beauty of the peninsula and its surroundings, and his dynamic promotional mind sparked thoughts of developing it as the "Atlantic City of the Pacific Coast".

He promptly teamed up with H.L. Chapin, of Portland, (who sold out early to Potter for a reported $100,000), and the two bought the 600-some acre peninsula lock stock and sandspit.

They platted 4,000 lots priced at $100 to $1,000 each

and laid out sites for construction of what they proclaimed to be the start of the finest residential-resort city on the Pacific Coast.

Miles of paved streets were designed to accommodate the town and provide scenic drives throughout the peninsula; this at a time when pavement was a rare thing on the west coast. Indeed, Tillamook City, the county seat and Tillamook County's largest town, had only mud and gravel for street surfaces.

To do the job, Potter and his associates built their own rock crusher and paving equipment.

Planning completed and construction started, the promoters launched one of the most grandiose sales-development campaigns ever hatched in the prolific mind of man, emblazoning periodicals with propagandized news stories and alluring display ads from coast to coast.

The *Oregonian,* Oregon's largest newspaper, in its issue of June 29, 1907, heralded the venture with the headline, "Portland Capitalists Plan Gigantic Beach Resort at Bayocean on Tillamook Bay".

The *Oregonian* article stated, "Commanding sites have been laid out for magnificent hotels, restaurants, dance halls, bowling alleys, golf links, tennis courts, baseball diamonds, stores and enchanting homesites."

The developers' original literature described the planned early construction of "the largest plunge in the world, 500 by 1,000 feet."

An elaborate natatorium when eventually completed contained a 50 by 160-foot pool, considerably smaller than originally planned but good-sized even by today's standards.

Potter and his associates must be credited with progressive ideas far in advance of their era, exemplified by descriptions of the well-equipped structures they did, indeed, build.

An article in an early 1900's issue of the *Tillamook Headlight,* stated, "The southern end of the plunge is an imitation of a waterfall over whose arranged boulders the water cascades and which is lighted by colored electric bulbs that show beautiful prismic effects.

"It is supplied with ocean water heated to the right

Elaborate Bayocean natatorium boasted a 50 by 160-foot pool, wave-making device, and a gallery capable of holding 1,000 persons. (From author's collection)

Tiny steam railroad installed by Potter and his associates was used as a segment of local transportation of Bayocean Peninsula. (From author's collection)

The yacht *Bayocean,* moored at Potter and associates' Bayocean dock, was used to transport persons between Bayocean and Astoria and Tillamook Bay points. (From author's collection)

temperature from pipes leading to the boilers in the engine room and is equipped with a band stand, gallery capable of holding 1,000 spectators, theater with motion picture equipment, several hundred dressing rooms and modern features throughout."

The pool's crowning highlight was "the latest wonder, a wave-making device creating artificial surf — so real in its action as to fool old Neptune himself".

The 40-room hotel was electric lighted, steam heated, equipped with automatic sprinklers for fire and boasted a spacious recreation room and an elegant dining room specializing in native sea foods.

An electric plant installed by the developers provided power for lights and equipment in the natatorium, hotel and other buildings in the city, and early in the development a gravity water system was installed to bring clear mountain water 3½ miles from Coleman Creek on Cape Mears.

Transportation in those days was cumbersome. The railroad to Tillamook had not been built, good roads were virtually non-existent, and no road connected Tillamook and other mainland areas to Bayocean Peninsula, though one was promised for the near future. The "near future" was not to arrive until 1928, when the road was finally completed.

To ease the problem Potter and his associates built docks and a luxurious yacht named *Bayocean*, which made weekly trips to Astoria to pick up train passengers from Portland and inland points for the 50-mile run down the coast from the Columbia River to Bayocean. It was also used to transport persons and supplies from Tillamook Bay points.

Promises by the promoters in 1907 that the Pacific Railway & Navigation Company's line would be completed by the next year, permitting "trains to run to Tillamook Bay in less than two and a half hours from the heart of Portland," did not materialize.

In spite of transportation difficulties, the public did buy lots, 2,200 of them at a gross income to Potter and associates of over $1 million, and about 100 buildings and homes were built — many of them elegant in design and appointments attesting to their millionaire owners.

The first noticeable erosion, about a foot a year on the peninsula's seaward side, started in 1917, the same year that construction of a jetty was completed on the north side of the Tillamook entrance channel opposite the north end of Bayocean Peninsula, prompting residents to suspect the jetty as the erosion cause.

But a subsequent report by the Beach Erosion Board of the Coastal Engineering Research Center in Washington, D.C., attributed the erosion to natural causes and discounted the jetty theory, stating, "When the ocean has reached its equilibrium, it will cease to erode."

But crashing breakers tore into the peninsula with mounting destructive force, gulping to oblivion massive chunks of sandy soil along with thick vegetation and deep-rooted trees, leaving homes and buildings vulnerable to the onslaught.

Erosion threat, overspending and inadequate travel facilities worried Potter to his demented self destruction and plunged the development into bankruptcy. Eventually the property and affairs of the T.B. Potter Realty Co. were consigned to receivership.

The town died hard.

Various groups and backers tried to pump new life into the development, and when in 1928 a road from

Before Peninsula was breached. Bayocean Peninsula, southerly end of spit, high tide 9 January 1951. (From author's collection)

After Peninsula was breached. Bayocean Peninsula, southerly end of spit, high tide 18 November 1952. (From author's collection)

Tillamook to Bayocean was finally opened with great fanfare, it was expected to be a sure cure for the resort's ills.

Bayocean did, indeed, enjoy a brief spurt of prosperity, cut short by the Great Depression of 1929 — and the ocean's onslaught.

Don Olson, erstwhile pianist and veteran Tillamook Bay-based commercial fisherman and charter vessel operator, recalls playing the piano for dances and entertainment at the Bayocean pavilion during a prosperous period. "It was a going institution then," he reminisced. "Crowds would flock to the resort from miles around.

"I was especially impressed with the beautiful homes and buildings, and I can tell you it was a shock while fishing off Bayocean during the following years to watch those same structures teetering on the edge of the surf-undercut bank; then crash into the ocean."

A 'Brief of the Bayocean Erosion' issued by the Tillamook Chamber of Commerce states in part, "In 1932 the erosion increased alarmingly . . . . . a choice area of ocean frontage, 100 to 200 feet in width and three miles long has been washed into the sea . . . . . roads, homes, business buildings, and natatorium were carried away and smashed to bits."

And still the ocean bored in.

An 1866 map showed the peninsula 600 feet wide at its narrowest spot at the southern end, and a 1938 map showed it only 260 wide at the same place.

Mr. and Mrs. Les Keenan, long-time Tillamook county residents, recall visiting Bayocean in the 1930's. "Three walls of the hotel were still standing," they remembered, "but its westerly side had collapsed into the sea. Most of the furniture and equipment was still in the building, and we plunked on a piano in a corner of the recreation room.

"During later visits we watched the entire hotel finally collapse into the ocean along with the tennis courts and several homes," they recounted.

"I remember a big home overhanging the bluff and while we watched a beautiful davenport and chair dropped into the sea," recalled Mrs. Keenan. "There was so much of that stuff never salvaged."

Left photo: Beverly Kunz amid remains of dead forest on west side of Bayocean Peninsula. (Photo by author)

Right photo: Trees lie against foot of embankment atop which they grew as part of healthy forest before being undermined by sea on west side of Bayocean Peninsula. (Photo by author)

Bottom photo: (Left to right) Linda Hall and Beverly Kunz examine shattered pavement from former Bayocean street system. Sea-shattered tree in background was once part of lush Bayocean forest. (Photo by author)

Bar-view Oregon, seeing a sudden end to its local hotel when nature took a hand during erosion that killed nearby city of Bayocean. (From author's collection)

In the winter of 1939 a vicious storm sent towering breakers crashing against the peninsula, gouging out tons of real estate along with several homes that had survived earlier onslaughts and tearing through its narrow southern end, washing out huge sections of Bayocean's access road and pounding on into Tillamook Bay.

Alarmed Tillamook County officials and citizens warned in a poignant report, "It is certain that ultimately there can be but one result — the breaking through of the Pacific Ocean into Tillamook Bay with the final result that the entire promontory will be swept away and Tillamook Bay would become a part of the Pacific Ocean, with the loss of all its industries and farm lands."

The breached peninsula's southerly end and access road were temporarily repaired with state and county funds, but plans for federal funds to construct a rockfill dike to permanently halt the ocean's threat were denied by the U.S. Army Corps of Engineers "because the Corps was unable to recommend expenditure of funds to save private property."

In the early 1940's about 20 die-hard residents stuck to their sea-threatened Bayocean homes, and in 1943 a carpenter named Lewis Bennett moved to the remnants of Bayocean and took over management of the water system. Like an umbilical cord the water from Cape Mears still pumped life into the dying town.

Bennett watched the town die violently in 1952.

An earthquake in Japan was the prologue to doom. Ten days after it struck, 5,000 miles across the Pacific, Bennett recalled the awesome sight of 50-foot seas charging out of the west and sledgehammering the shoreline, tearing out tons of soil along with trees and homes with every smashing inrush.

The hurtling seas ripped deep chasms through the peninsula's southern end, tearing out the road and water main and thundering on into Tillamook Bay.

Like rats leaving a sinking ship, the town's last residents struggled to the mainland by boat and across the breached access peninsula at low tide and never returned.

Fearful of catastrophic disaster should the Pacific continue to smash Bayocean Peninsula into obliteration and leave Tillamook Bay open to the sea, Congress in 1954 authorized the Army Corps of Engineers to start immediate construction of a 1.4-mile sand and rockfill dike along the southerly end of Bayocean Peninsula to close the breach and prevent further erosion. It was completed in two years and like the Dutchman's finger in the dike is holding out the sea.

Exploring Bayocean Peninsula afoot recently, this writer found no surviving signs of the town save the remains of a small roof and a short section of still-sturdy Potter-paved roadway.

The roadway ended abruptly in a jagged edge overhanging a sea-undercut embankment on the peninsula's westerly side. Scattered along the beach below, like pieces of a giant jigsaw puzzle, were shattered chunks of Potter's pavement — sadly symbolic of the developer's shattered dream.

The Bayocean breach at its worst, photographed on May 7, 1954. Breaks in the peninsula began in 1939, and finally reached a width at the ocean front, as shown, of about a mile, endangering the entrance channel to Tillamook Bay and eroding the inner bay shoreline. The Tillamook Bay North Jetty, constructed by the Corps of Engineers in 1917, can be seen at upper left. Tillamook Bay is to the right of the Bayocean Peninsula. (From author's collection)

Lower left photo: Jagged edge of roadway paved by Potter and associates in early 1900s overhangs sea-undercut embankment on west side of Bayocean Peninsula (foreground). Chunks of shattered pavement are strewn along beach below. (Photo by author)

Lower right photo: Beverly Kunz, standing on remaining short section of roadway paved by Potter and his associates in early 1900s, looks at remains of small roof, only surviving sign of man-made structures at former site of Bayocean (Photo by author)

7. Grounding of *Columbia River Lightship No. 50*

The first United States lightship on the Pacific coast was the *Columbia River Lightship No. 50*, stationed off the Columbia River mouth in 1892.

Built in San Francisco, she was wooden hulled, 123 feet in length and had a beam of 27 feet. She had no motive power and had to rely on sails for emergency use. Tugs were used to haul her to and from her station.

When she was torn from her anchorage in a violent southwest storm that raked the Columbia River mouth November 28 — 29, 1899, with towering seas and hurricane force winds, her sails proved futile.

After the efforts of tugs and the lighthouse tender *Manzanita* to take her in tow failed, she was hurled through raging breakers onto the sandy beach inside McKenzie Head on the River mouth's north shore.

At low tide Captain Joseph Harriman and his crewmen were able to walk ashore without injury. The ship was later hauled over a timber runway across nearly a mile of dry land with windlasses turned by horses to Bakers Bay, where she was relaunched sixteen months after grounding, towed to Astoria for repairs; then placed back on station, where she remained nine more years.

In 1909 she was replaced by the steam-powered *Columbia No. 88* which had been built at Camden, New Jersey, and steamed around Cape Horn to take over the post the doughty *No. 50* had guarded so long.

Artist's conception of Lightship *Columbia* toughing out storm on station.
(From author's collection)

Columbia River Lightship No. 50, carried ashore near McKenzie Head in 1899, is shown here being hauled across the spit on skids, to be relaunched in Baker Bay. (From author's collection)

8. Wreck of the *Enid III*

"Both engines out! Can't last much longer!"

The terse radio message stuttered through the receivers of half a hundred Pacific northwest Coast Guard stations and harbor-bound fishing vessels at 3:10 p.m., March 21, 1948.

For 24 hours coastguardsmen and fishing vessel skippers, straining to hear above the blast and scream of the 50-knot southwest gale that had been hammering the Oregon coast the past 30 hours, had remained glued to their radios in the desperate hope of getting a bearing on the missing 50-foot yacht, *Enid III*.

The Coast Guard radio station at Grays Harbor, Washington, which controlled all Pacific northwest emergency traffic, had intercepted confused reports from the *Enid* at scattered intervals throughout the storm-ravaged day, triggering a frantic sea search by the 180-foot Coast Guard cutter *Mallow*.

At 6:00 a.m. the previous day, March 20, skipper Everett Munson had unmoored the yacht from a Crescent City, California dock and headed onto the Pacific over long, lazy ground swells.

A dark mass of clouds scudding past overhead squeezed the early light down to a leaden haze as Munson, operating the vessel alone, churned past the sea buoy and set the automatic pilot on a northwesterly heading for the 400-mile haul to his Columbia River destination.

Four hours later a driving gust from the southwest lashed the yacht with a burst of rain, striking first warning of the approaching storm.

Steadily the wind built to a hammering 50-knot gale, blasting the sea's surface into a seething hell.

As she neared the 30-foot wide channel entrance, port engine failure causes *Enid* to broach onto rocks at north side. Note steam swirling from exhaust of still-running starboard engine. (From author's collection)

The voyage rapidly degenerated to a battering nightmare.

The automatic pilot would no longer control the plunging craft, and Munson was forced to remain at the bucking helm through 48 crashing, sleepless hours.

In mid-afternoon the starboard engine conked, and the vessel charged wickedly to starboard, heeling to leeward at a sickening angle.

Munson finally wrestled it out of the trough, and straining against the torque of the port propeller, held the careening craft to an offshore course.

"I knew I had to get one hell of a wad of sea room between me and shore," said Munson, "or I'd be on the beach in two whacks of a whale's tail if that port engine ever went out."

His judgment probably saved his life. At 2:45 p.m. the port engine quit.

Instantly the craft swung into the trough and commenced rolling crazily as gale and breaking seas hammered it broadside.

Gear and equipment were ripped from their moorings and slammed every which way.

Two 300-pound batteries tore loose from their housings and crashed onto the engines.

"Anybody says he don't get scared at a time like that is crazy as hell," Butch stated later. "I climbed down into the engine room, and it was like being inside a washing machine; gear and tools and water and loose things slamming all around. I knew I was done for.

"How in God's name I ever got those batteries re-set and hooked up, I'll never know. But I did, and I tried the transmitter and it worked. That was when I first hollered for help."

At 11:15 p.m. Chief Boatswain's Mate Francis Greenbrook, officer in charge of the Coast Guard station at Depoe Bay, pint-sized fishing port located on Oregon's rugged, rocky coast, 100 miles south of the Columbia River mouth, finally succeeded in getting two good RD bearings on the yacht, establishing its position as southwest by west of Depoe Bay.

The *Mallow* battled toward the radioed location and finally hauled alongside the battered yacht at 11:40 a.m., March 22, just as Munson, bruised and exhausted, got his engines restarted.

A veteran boat operator with 16 years experience, including countless crossings in and out of Depoe Bay, Munson declined the *Mallow's* offer to tow him to the Columbia River and decided instead to take the *Enid* into Depoe Bay.

"I was so bushed," he stated later, "I didn't figger I'd have the strength to bend their hawser to my bitt."

The *Mallow* escorted the yacht to the sea buoy, and Munson started his approach toward the narrow, breaker-bashed channel entrance a mile to the east.

Yacht *Enid III* shortly after hurled on rocks at Depoe Bay Channel entrance. (From author's collection

Coast Guard 36-foot motor lifeboat proceeds out Depoe Channel to pull yacht *Enid III* from breaker-bashed rocks. (From author's collection)

Maneuvering safely between 40-foot breakers on North and South reefs, a half mile offshore, he eased the plunging craft to the brink of Depoe Bay's crashing, 30-foot-wide channel entrance and started in.

Then it happened. The port engine quit in the instant he needed it most, for in that instant a roaring comber slammed against the laboring yacht's stern, broached it to port, and smashed it onto the rocks just north of the channel.

Chief Greenbrook fought his motor lifeboat alongside the pounding yacht, and with the assistance of Depoe Bay Coast Guard Auxiliarymen, got a towing hawser aboard and took a strain.

Seconds later a towering comber heaved the *Enid* clear of the rocks and plunged it into the channel, almost on beam's end.

Greenbrook rammed his controls to full ahead and snatched the smashed yacht into the harbor and safety.

Ruefully examining the drydocked *Enid's* smashed hull and fittings the following day, Munson voiced some strong recommendations for the benefit of sea-going yachtsmen.

"A man wants to make damn sure his fuel tanks, lines, and filters are clean before he takes his vessel to sea," he vehemently stated. "Engines that run fine in calm inshore waters can conk out cold, like the *Enid's,* from scale and crud jarring loose in rough water and clogging the system.

"Same with the bilge. It's gotta be cleaned slick as a seal's back, or the junk washed loose in heavy weather will clog the bilge pump, and you've had it. A vessel that's been used in inland waterways usually makes water hellishin' fast at sea. The above-water seams get dried out and cracked, and they gulp water by the gallon in ocean swells.

"All gear and fittings should be securely stowed, lashed, or bolted. Even a screwdriver can be a lethal missile when it's hurled across your craft by a driving beam sea.

"The Coast Guard forecast should always be checked before a vessel puts out, no matter how good sea and weather conditions appear. If I'd done that I'd never have been caught in that blow.

"If a boatman does get caught in a screamer, he should run before it and get a fistful of sea room between himself and the beach. Kept in deep water, the vessel will almost always bring him through.

"A yachtsman should never put to sea without at least one other person aboard to help him stand watch and assist in emergencies. Look at me. To save the few bucks I'd have had to pay a deckhand, I took the *Enid* out alone and cracked up to the tune of four or five grand.

"Hell, it's done now. I just hope other sea-going yachtsmen will take a lesson from me; so their cruises will be safe, not suicide."

9. The Ship That Committed Suicide

The blast of the 96-foot deep sea tug *Klihyam's* air horn bounced off the wooded slopes bordering Tongue Point and died in a ricochet of ghostly echoes along the lower Columbia River in Oregon.

One of the strangest epics in the history of West Coast seafaring had started.

The *Klihyam's* tow, the decommissioned U.S. Army transport *Joseph Aspdin,* was destined to give a big boost to the ancient sailors' superstition that ships have souls, for the 365-foot transport pulled about every foul maneuver known to mariners and finally committed suicide rather than end her days sunk in the mud as a dock revetment.

Veteran of World War II service, the *Joseph Aspdin* was one of a fleet of steel-reinforced concrete steamships built for the government at Tampa, Florida, in 1944. Since the end of the war she had been anchored with the U.S. Maritime Administration's mothball fleet in Cathlamet Bay, just upriver from the Tongue Point Naval Station at Astoria.

Early in 1948 the Yaquina Bay Dock and Dredge Company purchased the 5000-ton transport and contracted with the Sause Brothers Ocean Towing Company to tow her 132 miles down the coast to Yaquina Bay at Newport, Oregon, where she was to be stripped of her gear and sunk as a revetment for a new dock.

Captain Winthrop A. Rowe, at 29 a veteran of 12 years of Pacific Coast towboating, was selected to do the job with the tug *Klihyam.* He had a top record as a tug skipper. A fellow tug skipper called Rowe the "cattiest operator in the business".

The *Joseph Aspdin* (From author's collection)

A fantastic chain of events began when Rowe slacked the whistle cord and jotted in the rough log:

"1015, 14 March, 1948. Under way with *Aspdin*."

Rowe rang up Ahead Slow in the wheelhouse and watched astern as the bellying tow cable lifted from the waters of Cathlamet Bay. At the end of the cable the *Joseph Aspdin*, still wearing her drab grey war paint, eased slowly from her berth and was under way on her reluctant final voyage.

The *Klihyam's* 800-horsepower diesel engine roared into a noisy staccato as Rowe increased speed to Ahead Half.

The *Aspdin*, a white wave growing at her bow, gathered headway, then abruptly bumped to a stop.

Rowe rang up Ahead Full.

A frothing cataract boiling from her counter, the big tug strained on the tow line. No good. The *Aspdin* was hard aground.

Rowe radioed for assistance. Shortly three Maritime Administration tugs foamed alongside, were secured at strategic positions along the *Aspdin's* hull, and churned full bore against the transport.

At last the big ship sucked clear only to ground again and yet again.

"It sounds nuts," Rowe later declared, "but I'll swear that damned *Aspdin* seemed to have a will of its own and did everything in her power to keep from being hauled away."

After two tough hours, the straining tugs fought the *Aspdin* to Cathlamet Channel's confluence with the Columbia River. The maritime tugs cast off.

Rowe spoked the *Klihyam* to port and swung the tug down-channel against the flooding tide. As the *Aspdin's* ponderous bow plowed into the Columbia's powerful upriver tidal surge, it sheared hard to starboard in a sweeping rush and headed directly upriver on the direct opposite of its intended course.

Rowe rammed the annunciator to Ahead Full and black smoke geysered from the tug's stack.

"I looked over the *Klihyam's* bow and couldn't believe my eyes," stated Rowe. "Our stern wash was actually coming out from under the bow. The tow was pulling us backwards upstream."

"That ship had a mind of her own and she wasn't about to go to Newport!".

Rowe rang up Stop, ordered most of the tow cable winched in, and after considerable backing and filling finally got the *Aspdin* squared away on the downriver haul.

At 3 pm. the tug and tow hauled abeam of a Port of Astoria dock where the *Aspdin* was to be tied up for final sea preparations.

Rowe signaled for assistance, and shortly two tugs churned alongside and were secured to the *Aspdin's* port side. The two tugs started easing their unruly charge toward the slip. The ship started easily enough, but just before entering the slip she sheared to port, split a dolphin, and splintered a 20-foot gash in the end of the pier.

The tugs finally got the *Aspdin* into the slip and tied up at 4:30. Six hours to navigate six miles.

At daylight, March 26, sea preparations were completed. Rowe eased the tug and tow from the slip and swung to port for the 12-mile river run to the Pacific Ocean.

Steadied by a sea anchor trailing from her stern, the *Aspdin* followed handily till it plowed abeam of buoy 14, nine miles downriver. There it sliced to port, ran down the buoy and fouled it in the sea anchor.

Though slowed to a hard-won two knots, the sturdy *Klihyam* dragged the buoy-bedecked *Aspdin* — chain, seven-ton anchor, and all — three miles, almost to the river's mouth, before the 14-ton buoy finally cleared itself and dropped astern, the sea anchor with it.

Freed of the drag, the *Aspdin* surged viciously to starboard.

Rowe rang up Stop, straightened his tow. Power on her again, she sliced to port.

"Ring up stop . . . Back and fill . . . Straighten tow . . . Ahead slow . . . Ahead half . . . Rotten shear . . . Stop, dammit, ring up Stop!"

Rowe finally cursed his charge across the bar, cleared the lightship, six miles offshore, and pointed his bow south for the 120-mile pull to Yaquina Bay.

The *Aspdin* behaved like a lion on a leash, plunging first wide to port, then starboard; port, starboard; through two hectic days and nights of seagoing hopscotch.

Just after daylight on March 28, Rowe, red eyed and rantin', finally dragged his tow alongside Yaquina Bay buoy, two miles off the harbor entrance, and radioed for another tug to assist.

The 65-foot tug *S.J. Lovell*, from Yaquina Bay, hauled alongside and secured a line to the *Aspdin's* stern to help steady it.

Slowly, slowly, cautiously the tugs started their touchy tow toward Yaquina bar and entrance channel.

Old-timers were betting they'd never make it. The *Aspdin*, they pointed out, would be the heaviest tow attempt ever made into Yaquina Bay. At high tide her 26-foot draft would barely enable her keel to clear the channel's 20 foot mean-low-water depth.

A rotten shear, they warned, would ram her into the bar's flanking reefs, the jetties, the channel-spanning highway 101 bridge piers, or the Newport docks with their nested fleets of fishing vessels.

Foot by foot the two tugs worked the reluctant transport across the bar and between the jetties, where two harbor tugs joined the maneuver. Carefully the four craft eased the ship up the channel, through the harbor, and a mile up the bay.

There, a scant thousand yards from the destination that was to have been her final resting place, the *Aspdin* broached hard to port and rammed hard aground on a sandbar. The straining tugs could not free her.

Next day, the *Aspdin's* owners decided to put an oil barge alongside and lighten her by pumping fuel oil from her tanks. Harbor tugs, they reasoned, would then be able to free her on subsequent high tides.

The *Klihyam* was discharged and Rowe took her to sea.

But repeated salvaging attempts by the *Lovell* and harbor tugs during the succeeding days failed. The big — and final — push started the night of April 11.

Crewmen secured the *Lovell* and three harbor tugs to the transport and commenced pulling at 11 p.m., two hours before high tide. Three and a half hours of power pulling failed to budge her.

Now the tide was dropping and it was decided to make a new effort during high water the following night, April 12.

Leaving the *Lovell* and an oil barge moored alongside the *Aspdin*, all hands departed on the smaller tugs. Salvagers deemed it unnecessary to drop an anchor — an omission that was to prove disastrous.

Crewmen on the dredge *Natoma*, anchored a quarter mile away, were to maintain watch.

At 3 a.m. a *Natoma* crewman steered his launch through gathering mist to the *Aspdin*, found all secure, returned to the dredge.

A half hour later he again headed for the transport. The enveloping mist had squeezed visibility down to a few yards.

He worried the launch through the murky darkness for a half hour. Failing to locate the transport, he groped his way back to the dredge.

His "no ship" report was greeted by derisive hoots from fellow crewmen, who suggested he visit the nearest oculist. They were soon to swallow their taunts.

Unobserved by anyone, the fast-ebbing tide had undercut tons of sand from the transport's hull and swept it free.

At about 4:30 a.m., Robert Ryman, night watchman at the Bumble Bee Seafoods dock at Newport, a mile downstream from where the *Aspdin* had run aground, abruptly checked his dock pacing to stare through the now-lightening gloom, first in amazement, then admiration as the *Aspdin* with the *Lovell* and oil barge secured alongside slid past straight as a string down Yaquina channel.

"I know it sounds goofy," Ryman commented later, "but they were holding such a steady course I didn't have a thought but that there were people aboard the tug shovin' the ship. I thought to myself what an expert job they were doing with that one tug, what with all the trouble the four tugs'd had gettin' the same ship in."

At daybreak, an hour later, Capt. Gus Christensen stood outbound across Yaquina bar en route to the fishing grounds with his 50-foot dragger, *Hero.*

As he cleared the jetty heads he noticed through the watery, early-morning light the loom of a ship a half mile north of the channel, where no ship should be.

He highballed alongside and was astounded to find it to be the derelict *Aspdin.* The *Lovell* had broken clear and was adrift about a quarter mile to the west.

A quarter mile to the east crashing white water marked the rocky peril of Yaquina Reef. The oil barge had broken loose and drifted to the very edge of the reef. Gus gunned toward it, radioing Yaquina Bay Coast Guard as he went.

He boiled close aboard, and crewmen Stanley Scott leaped to the barge's heaving deck, heaved a line to the *Hero.* Gus took a strain.

As he fought the barge to deep water, the Coast Guard motor lifeboat slammed across the bar with *Lovell's* crewmen aboard and rushed them to their tug.

Meantime, the *Aspdin* had drifted perilously close to Yaquina Reef. Christensen and Scott cut the barge loose for the tug to take over and raced toward the transport.

A single light line hung over the *Aspdin's* stern. Scott grabbed it as the dragger surged alongside, climbed hand-over-hand to the heaving deck; then bolted toward the bow to get a tow line to the *Hero.*

As Scott raced down the deck, the transport lifted on a cresting sea and smashed down on the reef in a jolting crash.

"I crawled to a hatch and looked below," declared Scott. "A ten-foot rock had busted clear through the hull."

Down by the bow, a 10-foot hole gashed in her bottom, the *Joseph Aspdin* finds a last resting place, safe from lubbers. The photograph was taken a short time after the fleeing vessel grounded. (From author's collection)

Transport *Aspdin* broke up and died on Yaquina reef. Unmanned, the ship had sailed alone from the harbor in vain attempt to reach the sea. (From author's collection)

Pinioned to the reef the wounded ship lived another ten days. Then at mid-morning April 22 during a lashing southwest storm the *Aspdin* suddenly listed hard to port, broke in two, and died.

A portion of her broken hull is visible at low tide yet today, a breaker-bashed monument to the U.S. Army Transport *Joseph Aspdin,* the ship that committed suicide.

10. The Ship That Refused to Die

Hull down and all sails drawing, the 200-foot four-masted schooner *North Bend* came boiling toward the Columbia River lightship on January 15, 1928, inbound in ballast from Australia, where she had delivered a cargo of lumber.

Her signal flag requesting a pilot snapped from her signal halyard before the strong northwest wind that bowled her along with a foaming bone in her teeth.

Her taff rail log recorded a spanking twelve knots.

This anachronism in the dying age of sail had accounted well for herself under command of Capt. Theodore Hanson, a seasoned windjammer skipper who had crossed the Columbia River bar many times.

Captain Hanson was strongly aware of the hazardous nightmare the bar could become at this time of year, and he strained his vision inshore through his binoculars for the hoped-for sight of the approaching pilot vessel.

No pilot craft in sight!

Frowning at a threatening fog bank approaching from the northwest, he decided to risk all and sail her across the bar without a pilot.

The crew leaped eagerly to the rigging to obey his commands, anxious to get ashore after many weeks at sea.

The *North Bend* was skirting dreaded Peacock Spit when the wind abruptly died, leaving the schooner wallowing dead in the water, her windless sails drooping, drifting toward the spit.

Captain Hanson frantically shouted for distress signals to be hoisted and both anchors to be dropped!

The anchors would not grip in the shifting current and sand!

Schooner *North Bend* ashore near Peacock Spit at mouth of Columbia River. (From author's collection)

The ship was now drifting over the dreaded shoals lying directly off the spit.

Still no help in sight!

Then a heavy blanket of fog settled in, shrouding everything in sepulchral gloom!

Crashing breakers suddenly shattered the crew's awareness and the ship struck, was heaved free momentarily; then smashed to the sandy bottom again with a bone-jarring crash!

Through the terrifying night the ship withstood the pounding, and when morning light at long last filtered through the gloom, the Coast Guard cutter *Snohomish* and the doughty little tug *Arrow No. 3,* out of Astoria, boiled up to heaving line distance and succeeded in getting lines on her.

Muscling every ounce of power into the effort, they finally managed to free her.

Her freedom was short lived!

The towing cable parted, and the schooner was slammed back on the spit higher than ever.

Salvage efforts were abandoned and the *North Bend* was left to bleach her bones on the beach, as had scores of ships before her — they thought.

The schooner had other ideas!

One morning several months after she had grounded, observers noticed that her position had changed.

Her prow was pointing up river, and as the flood tides surged about her, breakers "bulldozed" sand away creating a pool around her hull.

As the days passed, inch by inch, foot by foot, the hardy schooner began moving through what had been a large impenetrable sandspit.

She was gradually moving in an easterly direction through her little self-made canal, away from the pounding breakers that had attempted to devour her.

On February 11, 1929, thirteen months after crashing ashore, she made her escape into the quiet waters of Bakers Bay — well to the east.

Tugs awaited her and she was towed to Youngs Bay at Astoria, given hull repairs, converted to a barge and hauled lumber for several years until tugboatmen were

Schooner *North Bend* ashore near Peacock Spit. (From author's collection)

forced to cut loose her tow line in a severe storm off southern Oregon, but she did not die until four crewmen were safely removed from her battered hull.

Periodicals far and wide told of the *North Bend's* self-liberating exploit, and Robert Ripley was so impressed that he featured it in his *Believe It or Not* — a fitting requiem to the schooner *North Bend* — the ship that refused to die.

North Bend stranded on Peacock Spit. January 5, 1928. (Oregon Historical Society, Neg. No. 71139)

North Bend on Peacock Spit — January 1928. She worked a channel thru the sands and floated in the river near the dock shown at the left in the picture. (Oregon Historical Society, Neg. No. 71139)

11. Death Held the Helm

A misty pall hung over the Pacific's heaving slate-gray surface as the merchant ship *Margaret Dollar* steamed along the northern Washington coast toward Juan de Fuca Strait on October 31, 1927.

On the freighter's bridge Captain H.T. Payne ordered extra lookouts posted as a precaution against collision danger in the heavily-traveled shipping lanes leading to and from the Strait, gateway to Puget Sound, British Columbia and the inside passage to Alaska.

His precaution was to result in discovery of one of the strangest and most grisly items of flotsam in recorded maritime history to be carried over 5,000 miles across the Pacific Ocean from Oriental to Pacific Coast waters by the Japanese current.

This powerful warm Pacific Ocean current, counterpart of the Atlantic Ocean's Gulf Stream, originates off the Philippines, where it is called Kuroshio — black stream. Flowing northward it skirts the east coasts of Taiwan and Japan at a rate varying from three to 32 miles a day.

Its giant sweep curves eastward off Honshu, largest Japanese island, swings close to the Aleutian Islands; then surges southeast along the coasts of southeastern Alaska, British Columbia and the Pacific Northwest, finally merging with the California Current.

Each year the Japanese Current deposits thousands of items of Oriental flotsam and jetsam on Pacific Northwest shores, where they are pounced on by beachcombers.

Prized gifts from the sea include such items as green, yellow and purple glass Oriental fishing floats, ceramic-

Derelict fishing vessel *Ryo Yei Maru* after she was towed to Seattle. (From author's collection)

like urns, bottles, boxes, boards, bamboo and bits of boat wreckage.

It fell to the lot of *Margaret Dollar* crewmen to sight the Japanese Current's most incredible cargo — an 85-foot, 100-ton derelict Japanese fishing vessel with a cargo of human bones and dead men.

Fifteen miles south of Umatilla Reef lightship, a lookout reported a small vessel off the starboard bow.

Captain Payne focused his binoculars on what he expected to be one of the many American fishing vessels that frequently troll in that area.

Abruptly he ordered a course change toward the vessel — the strangest craft he had ever seen in these waters.

Hove to alongside a few minutes later, the crew stared down at stark dilapidation.

The strange vessel's narrow hull reached forward to an overhanging, sampan-type bow. A wooden taff rail around the stern was supported by carved stanchions, like those of old-time sailing ships.

Shredded canvas hung from two battered masts. Yellowed, once-white paint peeled from the deckhouse and hull, both streaked with rust.

As the eerie craft rolled in the ground swell, the men could see a solid crust of barnacles below the waterline and seaweed streamers several feet long.

The deck was a litter of wreckage, amid which human bones, bleached and clean-picked, gleamed white in the murky light.

Faded black lettering on the transom bore the wording: *RYO YEI MARU*, Misaki.

Captain Payne ordered a boat lowered, and a crew soon made fast alongside the wallowing mystery craft.

As the men cautiously hauled themselves over the bulwark, the only sound that greeted them was the clatter of loose gear banging in the rigging as the vessel rolled. Somewhere below, a door rasped to and fro on rusty hinges.

The men picked their way forward; wrenched the hatches ajar; peered into the holds. Nothing there. They crept into the pilot house and found only an unmanned helm and musty emptiness.

Then they pried open the engine room hatch. A rusty, partially-dismantled two-cylinder gas engine was visible in the gloom. Oily bilge water sloshed from side to side, splashing over the engine and scattered tools on the floorboards alongside.

Tenseness gripped the men as they reached the hatch leading to the crew's quarters. When they forced it open an escaping wave of stinking foul air all but turned their stomachs.

Holding their breaths, they inched down the ladder, and found themselves in the dank murkiness of a tiny galley. In corroded kettles on a rusty stove they saw human bones.

Creeping aft they discovered tiers of wooden bunks, all empty — save two. There, huddled side by side, were the withered bodies of two dead Japanese.

The boarding party fled to their boat, returned to the freighter and reported their ghastly findings.

Captain Payne, following instructions radioed from Seattle, ordered a towing hawser secured to the derelict, and the ship resumed its course. For the first time in nearly eleven months *Ryo Yei Maru* was under way.

That night the *Margaret Dollar* arrived at Port Townsend, Washington, with her strange charge. Officials immediately boarded the derelict to search for some clue to the mystery.

"There is mute evidence of the clean-licked human bones, which clearly points to cannibalism," declared Dr. L.P. Seavey, U.S. quarantine officer, first official aboard.

On November 1, custom officers discovered in the pilot house a thin cedar board upon which Tokizo Miki, dying skipper of the ill-fated craft, had scrawled a meager record of events leading to the tragic end.

Translated by H. Kawamura, Japanese consul at Seattle, the rude log listed the names of the 12 crew members and pathetically stated: "We, the above named 12 persons, departed from Misaki, Kanawaga Prefecture, on December 5, 15th year of Taisho (1926). While at work fishing, a part of the engine was broken. Eight bushels of rice which we had on board has been exhausted. No ships have passed by us. All hope is gone and only death is to be awaited."

The officers also found nine envelopes in which Captain Miki had carefully placed a lock of each man's hair to be returned home for burial in the Buddhist temple, in accordance with Japanese custom. Locks of hair of two of the crewmen who had died the same day were in the same envelope.

On November 2, the craft was towed to Pier 41, Seattle, and it was there on November 4 that customs officers made the dramatic discovery of a diary describing events from the time the vessel set sail from Japan.

It was kept by Sutejiro Izwa until he died March 17, at which time it was taken over by Gennosuke Matsumoto, who was the last to die and whose body was found huddled alongside that of the captain. It is a revealing insight into the thoughts of men who faced inevitable death.

Translated by Consul Kawamura, it reads in part:

December 5, 1926, zero a.m. From Misaki harbor, we sailed on off Choji, on our eighth sailing.

December 9. Fishing with good result — taking 200 pounds red fish and four sharks and four other fine fish.

December 12. Ship's crank shaft broke early this day and we are helpless. We tried to hoist sails. But on account of strong west winds we could not sail as we desired. The ship drifted on out of control.

December 14. Snow is beginning to fall without wind. We decided we must use rice sparingly. While we were eating breakfast, we sighted in northern direction a ship of about 20 tons. We signaled them by raising our flag, but they were out of sight.

December 16. At 7 a.m. we sighted a T.K.K. steamer and thought at last the favor of God was upon us. We raised two flags and kindled fire on deck and made a great noise. But the steamer proceeded off our track.

We sighted a fishing boat at 10 a.m. in a southwesterly direction and we signaled in various ways in vain, as it was out of sight in 30 minutes.

West wind began to blow. We were drifting helplessly.

December 18. For 18 hours this day we sailed west. We rested at 4 p.m. and had conference. There was no hope of meeting a steamboat and we decided to head for Bonin Island (about 500 miles southeast of Yokahama) and try our luck in meeting a steamer there, but it would take three or four months to reach it.

December 19. West winds all morning. Waves running high and we drifted on west wind for 30 hours. We are headed for Bonin Island and we think how long it takes it to wash us there. If we are out of luck, out fate is ended.

December 20. A jewel north wind is blowing and everything O.K. When the westerly winds were blowing day after day the captain began to talk of taking big chance and heading for America. The crew objected to that plan.

December 21. We were helpless and drifting before the wind going west. We all worshipped Konpira (Japanese god of seafaring men) at the shrine. We drew lots which indicated west and so we headed west.

December 23. Boat still drifting. At 5 p.m. we caught a 160-pound fish. We almost despaired of sailing west, yet in going toward the east it would take four months to reach America. It is too late to hope to meet a boat, and it is not manly to wait.

December 26. Unable to head west, we have at last

turned toward the east. We have finally decided to risk all and head for America.

December 28. Drifting westward with heavy wind shoving at the stern. If this keeps up 10 days we may be carried to land. This day we caught bonita. We dried the fish to preserve them. The rice is giving out.

It is after midnight. As the captain is without definite course, his heart is filled with trouble. We dare not express to each other our innermost thoughts.

We prayed to Konpira and promised him that we would never again ask of him unreasonable. Even our deepest prayers do not draw pity from our angry god! Oh, Konpira! Have pity on us or we shall throw away thy charms. No — No — No — No — oh, let us not think such heresy!

Konpira is still there. He is for right and justice. The evil that we think is in our minds. Have mercy on us, oh, Konpira. We heed your warning and suffer in all humility. Please pity us and forgive us!

December 31. We are drifting again. This is the last of the year. Greetings and a happy new year to everybody! Pray God to help us.

January 1. New Year day, the sixteenth year of Taisho (the era fixed by the reigning Japanese emperor). We celebrated this day by mixing rice and red beans and enjoying the luxury of koya jofu (dried bean cakes). We confessed to each other many of our innermost thoughts — and then came night. At 7 p.m. we are again becalmed and drifting.

January 3. We have had three good days of weather and our spirits have been high as we celebrated New Year day for three consecutive days. But fear is in our hearts again — whither are we bound? The sea is all about us and we have no compass to guide.

January 4. Praise be to Konpira! He has sent us rain. We gathered it in canvases and shall hoard it as a miser hoards gold.

January 7. We are still groping our way about the sea. We have tried to set our course by the sun, but all is in vain. We drift, drift in an endless sea.

January 17. (Here the diarist stated tersely: "We have repaired our engine." Obviously he was suffering illusions, for no previous reference to repairs had been made, and the very next day he confided to his diary, "We are still drifting."

January 27. A ship! A ship! Happy madness seizes us as we sight a steamer. We build a fire — we wave, we shout, we dance — but, oh Konpira! The stranger does not see us and is gone over the horizon. Alas, again we are drifting we know not whither. The sea is mighty. Oh, Konpira, are you without mercy?

February 1. We caught one fish and ate it for dinner.

February 13. Sickness is upon us. Hatuzo Terada has lain in his bunk these past five days and is wasting away. We have caught more fish to eat. Yukichi Tsume Mitsu has hurt his leg and has taken to his bunk. Who shall be next?

March 5. Today at breakfast we had no food. (On the next day Captain Miki wrote the cedar-board message of despair).

March 9. Denjiro Hosai this day died of illness. Tsumetaro Naoye now sick. Big bird was caught. (It was later determined that the birds were caught on tuna hooks baited with human flesh).

March 17. There being no wind, we repaired the sails. Sutejiro Izawa died. (Izawa had kept the diary up till this time. Matsumoto continued it until his death.)

March 22. There appeared a seal. We thought we were not far from shore. Tsupiuchi became ill from several days ago.

March 27. Clouds and a southwest wind. As it was an adverse wind we drifted. Terada and Yokota died today. We caught a large bird.

March 29. Rain, North-northwest wind changed to south-southwest wind at 3 p.m. We are drifting average of four miles an hour on account of the strong wind. Tokichi Kuwata died at 9 a.m. and Tokakichi Mitani died during the night. We caught a shark.

(Now the diary shortens. Drifting, illness and death are the most common entries.

April 6. Tsunjiuchi died . . . April 14. Yukichi Tsunemitsu died . . . April 19. Yoshishiro Udehira died . . .

April 27. We have drifted 140 days now. Our strength

is gone. We are waiting for our time to come.

May 5. From morning to 6 p.m. it was clear. And I being ill, I could no longer stand at the wheel, but I had to guide the ship. I cannot lose my life.

May 6. Captain Tokizo Miki became very ill.

May 10. No clouds. Northwest wind. Hard wind and high waves. Ship adrift with rolled up sails. Ship speeding forward south-southwest. I am suffering of the captain's complaints. Illness.

This is the last entry written by the dying Matsumoto.

For nearly six months more the luckless craft was destined to drift unseen until sighted by the *Margaret Dollar*.

On November 3, Captain Robert Dollar, president of the Dollar Steamship Company, telegraphed Consul Kawamura expressing sorrow at the calamity, disclaiming all salvage rights, and offering to return the craft to the Japanese owners on the deck of the S.S. *President Madison*, with the recommendation that proceeds from the sale of the vessel go to the families of the dead fishermen.

The families telegraphed a reply declining the offer; for, they said, the evil spirits aboard the bewitched ship would cause an exodus of the inhabitants from the village where she was owned.

She was cursed by Konpira from the moment she was launched in the spring of 1926, they lamented, for she was the first ship of her kind to flaunt tradition, being the first "great ship", five times the size of the vessels that had been used by Japanese fishermen throughout the centuries.

To offset the wrath of Konpira, on her maiden voyage her crew sailed her 250 miles down the coast to Konpira's shrine, where the ancient ritual of dedicating the vessel to the god was scrupulously observed.

It was to no avail.

On November 3, the two withered bodies were cremated, and on November 7 black-robed Chyosui Ike, Buddhist priest, chanted last rites before an improvised, incense-burning altar in a Seattle mortuary. On the altar were the weathered cedar board with its scrawled message of lost hope, an urn containing the ashes of the two bodies, and nine small envelopes with the locks of hair.

The death ship's doomed career ended December 19 when she was towed to Richmond Beach, on Puget Sound north of Seattle, soaked with oil and burned — intact.

Morbid irony is revealed in the translation of the vessel's name. *Ryo Yei Maru* means Good and Prosperous.

12. "A Breaker Was Busting Over Her"

A steep, green sea heaved the thirty-six-foot troller *Cara Lou* to its frothing crest, then dropped it into the yawning trough beyond. The sea had been building steadily all through that cloud-shrouded October fourth in 1936, and as the watery, late-afternoon sun crawled toward the ragged horizon, a gray pall of fog began settling over the Pacific's heaving surface off Depoe Day.

Aboard the *Cara Lou*, Skipper Roy Bower hurriedly hauled in his salmon-trolling gear, housed the outriggers, and shoved the throttle ahead. Smashing through curling crests and plunging troughs, the *Cara Lou* clawed alongside the wallowing sea buoy, where Bower set his course for Depoe Bay's channel entrance, a mile to the eastward.

Holding to a deep-water course between thundering combers on North and South reefs, he maneuvered his bucking craft to the breaker-bashed channel entrance, waited for the flat spot between rushes, then skillfully snaked the vessel through the channel's churning hundred-yard length to the quiet safety of the tiny harbor.

He quickly tied the *Cara Lou* to the dock and hurried to the channel-spanning Highway 101 bridge to watch anxiously with fellow fisherman, Jack Chambers, as all but one of the vessels of the Depoe Bay fishing Fleet churned into the channel to the safety of the harbor. The twenty-five foot troller *Norwester* was still at sea.

As Bower and Chambers stared into the gathering fog, their anxiety deepened, for they knew that if the frail craft didn't reach port soon, it would be trapped by fog and darkness in the mounting seas.

They also knew that on board the imperiled troller

Storm warning hoist on weather mast at Depoe Bay. (Photo by author)

was not only its skipper, McQueen, but also two fourteen-year-old boys; Walter McQueen, the skipper's son, and Gene McLaughlin, a guest. Abruptly Bower pointed to a spray-drenched blur that was the *Norwester*, laboring toward the sea boy. Then the fog swirled onto the ocean's surface in a black mass, blotting out all vision.

"Let's go!" yelled Bower. Chambers was already on his way. They raced down the steps to the dock, started the Cara Lou's engine, cast off and slammed through the surging channel toward the position where they'd glimpsed the *Norwester*. Fifty feet offshore the fog swallowed them.

McQueen described the tragic events that followed:

"I had tied to the sea buoy and was going to ride it out there till morning. All of a sudden the *Cara Lou* comes busting out of the fog, and Bower and Chambers holler at me to cast off and follow them in.

"I cut loose and followed them on a northeasterly heading for about five minutes. The seas kept getting steeper and steeper, and then one big one busted clean over my vessel and broached us broadside.

"I'll never know how we missed capsizing, or how that danged engine kept running, but we slammed out of it in one piece and I headed back to the sea buoy and tied up. It was dark then with a black-out fog.

"Last I saw of the *Cara Lou* she had swung beam-on to the seas and a breaker was busting over her. I didn't know till I came in next morning that Bower and Chambers hadn't made it. God, I wish I could have done something to help."

When neither vessel returned to port that night, fishermen aboard other vessels attempted to batter their way to sea through the rampaging channel to search for the missing vessels but, each time, the thrashing combers clubbed them to a standstill, and they were barely able to get back to the safety of the harbor. Then the tide dropped below navigable depth, shutting off further search attempts.

Throughout the black night, fishermen and townsfolk patrolled the rocky shoreline in the hope of spotting or hearing something. By the next morning the sea had moderated, but the cotton-wool fog still clung to the sea's dark surface.

Suddenly, anxious watchers on the highway bridge heard the stutter of a boat's engine and a hazy blur grew to the little *Norwester* struggling toward the channel entrance.

McQueen wrestled his plunging craft through the channel to the harbor and tied up.

Fishermen pounded down the stairs to the dock, informed the shocked McQueen that the *Cara Lou* had not returned, got a quick report of where he'd last seen the missing vessel, and got underway in their own vessels to fan out over the Pacific's fog-shrouded surface in a desperate search.

They found the battered hulk of the *Cara Lou* drifting awash two miles northwest of Depoe Bay. Bower's body was aboard, tangled in the rigging. Chambers was floating nearby in a life preserver. He had died from exposure.

A few days later, fishing vessels carried relatives and friends of the drowned fishermen onto the Pacific, where their ashes and flowers were scattered on the water in a brief ceremony.

Later, Bower and Chambers were posthumously awarded the Carnegie medal for heroism. The state of Oregon erected a native stone monument overlooking the Pacific in Depoe Bay in tribute to the heroic fishermen.

The author beside stone monument overlooking the Pacific at Depoe Bay, erected by the State of Oregon in tribute to fishermen Roy Bower and Jack Chambers, who gave their lives in an effort to assist a storm-imperiled fellow fisherman. (From author's collection)

13. Rum Runner

A murky sun was hauling itself over the forested rim of the coastal mountains east of Vancouver Island as three Canadian rumrunners — Stanley Babcock, Charles Ryall and William Kerr — eased the *Sea Island* from their Victoria, British Columbia, dock, cleared the harbor and headed westward down Juan de Fuca Strait.

The date was February 1, 1932; their destination, Whale Cove, Oregon where they were to rendezvous with a coastwide gang of rumrunners to whom they would deliver the fortune in illicit alcohol, — whiskey and rum they'd spent all the previous night stowing in the *Sea Island's* hold. Late that afternoon they churned past Swiftsure Bank Lightship, which guarded the entrance to Juan de Fuca Strait, and swung their pitching craft south, heading into gusty headwinds and choppy seas.

Holding well offshore to avoid interception by patrol craft of the United States Coast Guard, they slugged their way slowly down the coast, raked by cresting seas and gale-force winds. Finally, just before darkness enveloped their plunging craft on Sunday night, February 7, the exhausted rumrunners made out Cape Foulweather's jutting promontory, which they knew was just south of Whale Cove.

They swung east and — staring through binoculars into the roiling murk ahead — at last made out the flickering yellow lights of the two lanterns the shore gang had hung on the "signal tree" on Whale Cove's easterly side. As they beat their way to the brink of the cove's breaker-lashed entrance, two of the rumrunners yelled a warning to the skipper that he was too far south and headed for the rock in the south side of the entrance.

Author's charter vessel *Tradewinds Kingfisher* in Whale Cove. (Photo by Fredrick Stanley Allyn)

While the skipper was shouting at them to mind their own blankety-blank business — he knew what he was doing . . . . Crash! A roaring comber slammed the embattled vessel against the rock, holing the hull and starting a fire in the engine room. They were barely able to get the skiff clear in the thrashing turmoil and make it to the beach.

The breakers soon extinguished the fire and the *Sea Island* with its illicit cargo was hurled onto the beach.

When the gang was spotted ditching the booze next morning, most of them scattered and hid out till the heat was off. The three men from the *Sea Island* sped north up the coast highway in a stolen auto provided by the shore gang. At Hebo, forty miles north, bad luck struck again. The car hurtled off the highway and overturned. None were injured and they boarded a bus for Portland, a hundred miles inland.

Later a state police officer, investigating the wrecked automobile, noticed that its license plates had been switched. Learning that its occupants had boarded the Portland-bound bus, he phoned Captain Gurdane of the state police at Portland.

Gurdane arrived at the bus depot just after the bus

had pulled in and arrested the three Canadians as they were hopping a cab. They admitted being from Vancouver, British Columbia, and were held at Portland police headquarters for immigration authorities.

Meantime, Lincoln County, Sheriff McElwain and his men loaded the contraband liquor onto trucks, hauled it to Toledo, and stowed it in a storeroom in the Lincoln County jail to be held as evidence. On the wrecked rumrunner they discovered evidence linking the three Canadians to the affair. Questioned in Portland, the Canadians admitted their guilt and were jailed to await trial.

But the most fantastic phase of the affair was yet to come. Shortly after midnight on Sunday, March 20, 1932, two trucks, a sedan and a coupe pulled up in front of the Lincoln County jail at Toledo. Two men in the coupe, armed with machine guns, stood guard while the seven men in the other vehicles hustled a portable cutting torch from one of the trucks, cut through three steel jail doors and a lock on the storeroom door, and loaded the liquor being held as evidence onto the trucks.

When the heist was completed, the trucks, convoyed by the sedan, sped off toward Portland. The armed coupe and its occupants, presumed to be the big bosses of the gang, were never found.

Discovering the jail hijack later that morning, sheriffs and state police fanned out over the highways but came within a squeak of being completely foiled by the hijackers. A final bad break finished the fantastic event.

Near Grand Ronde, thirty-five miles east of the coast, the larger of the two trucks ran low on fuel and both trucks were forced to stop while fuel was transferred from one to the other. Officers drove up while this was going on and arrested the four men manning the trucks — Nels Krueger, George Fisher, Elbert Johnson and Arthur Adams.

Two of the officers, dressed in plain clothes, drove on with the trucks as decoys. A few minutes later, spotting the convoy sedan returning in search of the trucks, they quickly parked and when the sedan stopped alongside they leveled their guns at its occupants.

With hands held high, Burt Chapin, Sydney Carrick,

Paul Remaley and the three Canadians, who'd been sprung on bail, gave up without a struggle. Several guns and saps found in their vehicles were confiscated, along with the vehicles and liquor.

All were sentenced to fines and penitentiary terms on charges ranging from destruction of public property and theft of government evidence to transporting and having in possession, while armed, alcohol and moonshine whiskey in violation of the National Prohibition Act.

When Prohibition was repealed on December 5, 1933, pending indictments against the prisoners were dismissed.

14. Free Roams the Gray Whale

Dead ahead — barely a boat's length — forty tons of gray whale erupted through the Pacific's gently heaving surface as the huge mammal exploded from the depths in a cyclone of spray. For a split second the monster hung poised thirty or more feet above us, his great jaws gaping, his tremendous tail beating the ocean's surface.

I slammed the engines astern and for a heart-stopping moment thought they were going to conk, but they caught and as we backed off, the whale crashed sideways into the sea with a tidal-wave whack.

September of this year had coasted in with clear, warm "Indian summer" weather. Just ten minutes earlier we had cleared the Depoe Bay channel on a salmon trip and had churned west along the path blazed by a bright sun. But after our near collision with the leviathan, we hove to and watched while it leaped clear of the sea a half dozen more times, then disappeared beneath the surface.

A few minutes later it showed farther south, its mate alongside, their spout spray puncturing the surface, followed by their broad gray-black backs rolling from the sea, then submerging in a series of shallow dives. Finally the behemoths thrust their ten-foot-wide, twin-fluked tails high and plunged to the depths.

These two huge mammals turned out to be the vanguard of the tremendous six-thousand-mile migration of Pacific gray whales that takes place along the Oregon coast each fall, winter and spring, as it has for centuries. I had heard about this great migration, but actually witnessing its start spurred me to dredge every scrap of information I could about gray whales from writings about

Surfacing, spouting Gray Whale. Note twin blow holes (nostrils). (Photo by author)

Powerful up-and-down strokes of whale's ten-foot tail drive it to the depths at start of its deep dive. (From author's collection)

Gray Whale at start of deep deep dive. (Photo by Tim Buehler)

them and from talking to fishermen and others with knowledge about them and their antics.

Through my following years at sea I bulwarked my whale knowledge by chasing and pacing the giant mammals at as close range as prudent. Though a few grays show up as early as September, the bulk of the pods do not appear until December and January. From then until March they surge southward in almost continous procession, their backs, tails and spout spray visible close offshore almost any hour of the day.

Traveling in pods of two to ten or more, they scull their boxcar-size bodies through the sea at an average four-knot clip for a fifteen to twenty-hour day, taking three to four months for the long migratory haul. When pursued by ships or natural enemies, grays have been clocked at a ten-knot speed for an hour or more, and to attain sufficient speed to leap from the sea they can accelerate to thirty knots, according to authorities.

The huge grays propel themselves with up-and-down strokes of their powerful horizontal tails — unlike fish, which have vertical tails. They steer with their flippers, which project as much as fourteen feet from each side of their body. Alternately surfacing, spouting and sounding, they periodically heave their immense tails high in the air at the start of their deep-sounding dive, followed by a ten to fifteen-minute submerged stint.

Their southward migration originates in their summer feeding grounds in the Gulf of Alaska, the Bering Sea and the Arctic Ocean. Their winter feeding, mating and calving grounds are in the bays and lagoons along the western shore of Baja California and the eastern side of the Gulf of California. Scammons Lagoon, a 250-square-mile body of water, 350 miles south of San Diego, is their principal winter habitat.

The lagoon is named after the famous whaling shipmaster, Captain Charles Melville Scammon, who took command of the brig *Mary Helen* in 1852, prowled the lagoon as his favorite hunting ground, killed hundreds of whales there and became an authority on whales and their habits.

No one knows how long these gray-whale migrations

have been taking place — probably for many eons. Spanish sea captain Sebastion Viscaino, sailing up the Oregon coast in the vicinity of Cape Blanco, noted in his log for one day in 1603 that they had sighted huge numbers of whales. That was seventeen years before the Pilgrims landed in America.

An adventurous group recently tried to record the heartbeat of a gray whale off the west coast of Baja California, hopeful of learning something more about heartbeat in general. They failed to get accurate timed beats, but deduced that the gray's heart beats only five or six times a minute, compared to the Arctic white whale's twelve to fourteen times a minute. Heartbeat of tiny mice runs from three hundred to six hundred times a minute. Heartbeat slows down as animals become larger.

Whales have huge brains and they know how to use them, as I found out while on a whale-watching cruise a while back about three miles southwest of Depoe Bay. We were pacing two big southbound grays at about 100 yards distance and my passengers lined the port rail "oo"-ing and "ah-"ing and taking pictures.

Suddenly the big mammals changed from a southerly to a due easterly heading, then sounded.

Not to be outsmarted by two mere whales, we too changed to an easterly heading and cruised that course past where the whales had sounded, waiting for them to resurface.

At long last their twin spouts showed — a good mile to the south on their original heading and clear out of our range.

You can't tell *me* those whales didn't turn east then sound just to get rid of us; then, safely shut of us, they turned south while submerged and resumed their original course.

Gray whales prefer shallow water, often swimming in the surf. I have seen them actually, scraping their ponderous sides against breaker-bashed rocks during their close inshore journey along the Oregon coast. A while back, Depoe Bay resident, Lavelle Connell, reported seeing a gray whale surface directly under the bell buoy, a half mile west of the Depoe Bay channel entrance.

"I saw it submerge close to the buoy," she declared. "Then suddenly the buoy rose into the air, leaned way over, and crashed back into the sea, rocking crazily, its bell clanging like mad."

Fishermen aboard vessels anchored at night have told of being startled awake by harsh, scraping noises against their anchor cables, accompanied by pitching and veering of their vessels. They attribute the disturbances to whales.

It is thought by many that whales' scraping antics are for the purpose of removing barnacles and crab-like whale lice which dig deeply into battle-incurred sores and cuts. Occasionally one of the beasts will run itself aground, as was the case with a forty-foot gray dubbed "Smelly Nellie," which committed suicide on the beach at North Cove in outer Depoe Bay in April, 1951, to the olfactory consternation of the local populace.

During a recent trip off Depoe Bay, the grays were rolling and spouting on all sides of my vessel, and as one mammoth brute rolled close aboard and snorted his odorous spray across our decks, a passenger from New York voiced the question that is put to me constantly, "Aren't they apt to ram a boat and smash it to smithereens?" Except for wounded whales, the answer is "no."

I have watched from the deck as a giant gray drove up from the depths like a surfacing sub to explode from the sea not twenty feet from my vessel. It swelled its great nostrils (blow holes) to geyser a cloud of warm, stinking vapor over us, then sounded without giving us a second look.

Several times I have gaped horrified, braced for the crunch, as surfaced whales headed dead center for our hull, only to watch them gracefully submerge at the last minute, swim under the hull without so much as a scrape, then surface on the other side.

As far as I know, not once has an unmolested whale attempted to attack my vessel or any others in this area. With wounded whales, or whales being attacked, it's different. In the heat of attack they could ram and damage or sink a small craft in their frantic twisting, turning, leaping attempts to shake off their tormentors.

Whalers capture the whales by firing a harpoon from

a cannon mounted on the bow. The harpoon head is filled with a bursting charge of powder, and the explosion scatters shrapnel-like metal pieces through the whale's body, killing it instantly. Occasionally the harpoon head fails to detonate; and then the whaler has a wound-maddened mammal on the end of his harpoon cable.

A few years ago, when whaling for some species was legal in United States waters, friends of mine had a close call while whaling off the northern California coast, in a wooden converted World War II minesweeper. The gunner fired a harpoon into a big whale, but the head failed to detonate.

The crew watched helplessly as the monster charged off, burned out the winch brakes, ripped the heavy harpoon-tethered cable from the smoking winch to the bitter end, and snapped it like thread.

As the crew stared, the whale, trailing the long cable, began swimming in a mile-diameter circle around the whaler. Deciding they could fire a second hastily readied harpoon into the whale, capture it and recover their gear, the men eased their vessel toward the circling behemoth.

Before they came within firing range, it suddenly broke off its circling course, charged straight at the whaler, smashed into the side of the hull with a splintering crash, turned aft under the keel, bent both shafts, propellers and rudders, and thrashed off.

Crewmen barely got water-tight doors dogged down in time to prevent sinking, and limped to San Francisco on one engine for emergency repairs.

Crippled whales have often been known to plunge to the depths, ripping a thousand fathoms of cable from the windlass and snapping it like trout line at the bitter end. On one occasion a blue whale, shot with a harpoon that failed to detonate, towed the whaling vessel at eight knots for seven hours before giving up.

Wounded sperm whales are the most dangerous of the beasts. They have a gigantic head, which they use as a ram, and they have been known to smash into and crush the hulls of five-hundred-ton vessels.

During their long migration journey of three to four months, gray whales feed on such things as plankton, squid and fish. In areas where crustaceans are abundant they bottom feed by bulldozing huge furrows across the ocean floor with their lower jaw and scooping up crabs, shrimp, clams and anything else in their path.

When they have a mouthful, they close their great jaws, and with piston-like thrusts from their huge tongues (that weigh as much as three thousand pounds) they squish water and sediment out through the strainer-like bony baleen that lines their mouths. Then they lick the remnants from the baleen, swallow the food into their four-chambered stomachs, and chow is down.

Like all mammals, the grays have lungs. They must surface to breathe every four to fifteen minutes through twin blow holes atop their heads. The spout spray that whale watchers see is vapor caused by warm air expelled from the whale's lungs into the colder sea air.

Like all baleen whales, the grays do not have teeth; they thrash their mighty tails, their only weapon, to ward off enemies. Their greatest enemy, until recently, was man.

In 1791, seven ships of the New England whaling fleet sailed around Cape Horn on the first whaling venture in Pacific coast waters. By chance they sailed smack into the gray whale migration, from which they reaped a rich harvest.

Their return to New England with a fortune in whale oil spurred increasing numbers of Atlantic whalers into beating around the Horn to Pacific coast waters. In 1847, the "golden year" of American whaling, more than five hundred of the six hundred New England whaling ships plied Pacific waters.

Toll among the grays was tremendous. The species was slaughtered almost to extinction, making whaling for them unprofitable during the latter part of the nineteenth century. With the cessation of whaling the gray population gradually increased, and in the 1920's and 1930's, whaling for them was resumed. Again their numbers were seriously depleted.

U.S. Fish and Wildlife Service counts show that grays were down to less than two hundred in 1930, a far cry from the thirty thousand estimated by Captain Scammon to be in Pacific coast waters in the middle nineteenth century.

Alarmed whaling nations went into belated action. In 1937, the United States enacted a law prohibiting the killing of gray whales, and in 1938 they were given complete protection by international treaty, which forbids the killing or taking of grays except by aborigines who use them as a food staple. In 1970, the fifteen-nation International Whaling Commission recommended that the prohibition on commercial hunting of gray whales remain in effect indefinitely.

Results are encouraging. Counts from shore and the air have shown an increase of about eleven percent per year. The gray population is estimated to number up to eighteen thousand at this writing.

Federal agencies have gone even further to protect the world's dwindling whale population. In 1970, the Interior Department put eight species of whales on the endangered species list, and early in 1971 the Department of Commerce banned the killing of any and all whales by any fisherman operating from U.S. ports, thus virtually putting an end to the three hundred-year-old U.S. whaling industry. That same year the Mexican government declared Scammons Lagoon a sanctuary for all wildlife in and around the lagoon, including whales. Thus their winter habitat remains safe and there they feed and breed and give birth to their calves until early spring, when they again churn to sea to start their northward migration.

It is thrilling to watch them roll and spout as they migrate along the coast in their mysterious sea world and it is exciting to get a close look at one of them that has come ashore and died in the land world. But, here, caution must be used, as U.S. Army Lieutenant Phil Sheridan found out the hard way while he was stationed in the Oregon territory in pioneer days . . . .

Word reached him of a battle being waged by two rival Indian tribes over division of a monstrous and very dead whale that had come ashore on an Oregon beach. Galloping to the scene with some of his troops, the lieutenant swung from his saddle and strode sternly up to the whale, his drawn sword flashing.

Dazzled by the splendor of this cavalry officer, the Indians ceased their battling and listened in awed silence as the lieutenant explained how the division was to be made. To emphasize his point, he raised his sword high above his head and brought it swishing down to mark the division in the whale's belly.

A mighty outrush of gas hit him full in the face and he passed out cold. Two of his troopers dragged him off a safe distance, and the Indians resumed their fighting — with the lieutenant a meek and groggy bystander.

15. Sea Creatures — Weird, Phantasmic and Mysterious

Sepulcher gloom hung over the sea's oily-calm surface creating an eerie atmosphere where we were trolling for salmon about five miles southwest of Depoe Bay.

A hazy mist squeezed visibility down to about one-eighth of a mile.

My anglers — twelve Lincoln City businessmen — talked in subdued tones, reflecting the somber mood created by the elements.

Gazing aft over the anglers' heads to watch for salmon signs, I suddenly became aware of a monstrous black something barging across our stern from west to east about an eighth of a mile out at the limit of my visibility in the edge of the mist.

What's *that?* I shouted, gesticulating excitedly.

One by one the anglers stood for a better view and remained, gaping trance-like.

We could discern neither head nor tail nor fins on the monster; just a smooth black back, like India rubber, some forty feet in length.

It plowed straight through the water, neither veering to right nor left or sounding, surfacing or spouting like a whale would. At its blunt forward end it shoved a huge bow wave, and at its after end it created a V-shaped wake.

As the creature vanished in the fog I stammered to my excitedly chattering anglers that I'd circle to port on a course that would intercept the creature.

But it vanished and we never saw it again.

And I've got witnesses, twelve of them — all solid Lincoln City businessmen!

While we were trolling on one trip a monstrous head

Author with 43½ lb. Chinook. (Photo by Rich Allyn)

Curious Hair Seals surface alongside charter vessel off Depoe Bay. (From author's collection)

Jodi Magher examines eight-foot elephant seal that beached itself and died near Depoe Bay. Elephant seals attain a length of sixteen feet, weight of over two tons. (Photo by author)

suddenly popped from the water alarmingly near us, and we found ourselves under the scary stare of a weird-looking brute with an elephant-like trunk. I later learned that it was an elephant seal, which is the largest of all seals and grows to sixteen feet in length, twelve feet in girth, and weighs up to five thousand pounds.

Several times we surged close to huge silver-gray cartwheel-shaped fish lying on their barn-door sized sides on the surface, their puckered mouths gaping open and shut. They proved to be ocean sunfish, which lie on their sides on the surface feeding on microscopic organisms and attain a weight of a ton, another of nature's anomalies.

While heading offshore on another fishing trip, about a mile offshore from us, we spotted what appeared to be a raft with some living thing perched on one end. We cruised to within a few yards of it and gaped in awe at an immense marine turtle, which normally inhabits tropical seas.

I later found that it is the largest living species of leathery marine turtle, which reach a length of eight feet and a ton in weight, and occasionally venture from tropical to northern waters.

Reports of giant sea serpents and monsters I am inclined to discount as stemming from optical illusions or the transfer of large amounts of alcoholic beverages from bottles to sighters' stomachs.

From a distance the serrated backs of surfacing whales resemble huge, undulating serpents as they alternately roll from the sea and submerge. A column of porpoises swimming single file appears the same. Even columns of birds such as shearwaters flying close to the surface appear to undulate like a serpent as they rise and dip over the waves.

Many times at sea I've investigated "sea serpents" and "monsters", only to find them to be gnarled oddly shaped logs and other drifting objects appearing much like grizzly monsters raising and lowering their craggy heads as they heave and roll in the swells.

Several times I've checked out mysterious "periscopes" bursting from the sea "for a look" then submerging. They turned out to be deadheads — waterlogged logs floating vertically, alternately ramming from the sea and disappearing beneath the surface.

Beauty and the beast. (Photo by Terry Thompson)

Skate held by Rich Allyn, skipper, and Tom Getty, mate,
aboard charter vessel *Sunrise.* (Photo by Val Allyn)

Octopus caught by skin divers in front of author's home. (Photo by author)

Depoe Bay fisherman, Bill Church, told about spotting a "monster surging in his direction while he was fishing off the northern Washington coast. When it got close, it proved to be two sea lions supporting a bleeding, injured third sea lion between them as they swam inshore toward a rocky sea lion habitat.

Veteran commercial fisherman, Mauri Pesonen, endured a frightening experience while salmon fishing off Depoe Bay. He had just landed a salmon in the fishing cockpit aft when a huge bull sea lion catapulted from the water in pursuit of the boated fish and crashed into the cockpit beside him. He barely scrambled clear, grabbed his rifle from the wheelhouse and shot the lion dead.

Ratfish caught by angler on ocean floor aboard charter vessel off Depoe Bay. (Photo by Tim Buehler)

Try as he might, he was unable to muscle the beast from the cockpit, so was forced to haul in his gear and return to port. The sea lion was hoisted clear with a dock crane and tipped the scales at eighteen hundred pounds.

The strangest creature discovered in the Depoe Bay vicinity was the three-thousand-pound sea monster dubbed Old Hairy, which washed shore near the mouth of the D River, twelve miles north of Depoe Bay, in April, 1950. Equipped with feathers and hair and an appendage measuring sixteen feet in length, it made world-wide headlines, piqued the curiosity of oceanographic scientists the world over and defies identification to this day.

The giant squids, which lurk in various areas of the oceans, are equipped with ten arms, instead of eight as in an octopus. Two of the tentacles are longer and more mobile than the other eight and extend out ahead of the body and are used for capturing prey, transferring it to the mouth and grasping it while it is being crunched in the horny jaws, which are situated around the mouth in the center of the circle of arms.

The Smithsonian Institute in Washington, D.C., has on display a mounted giant squid that measures over sixty feet to the tips of its outstretched forward tentacles.

An improbable creature called the flying squid inhabits mostly tropical seas. Its flight is a series of leaps across the surface of the sea, which are often strong enough to land it on the deck of a ship.

Disbelief gripped me as I stared at the Pacific Ocean edge where the breakers slam against the rocky shore in their last show of defiance before succumbing to the Oregon coast after rolling unchecked across the North Pacific from Hokkaido, Japan, five thousand two hundred ninety six miles to the west.

Before my gaping stare, one, two, three, four huge *yellow* tentacles came snaking up out of the turgid water, their upper portions thrusting about this way and that as though searching for something.

I stood transfixed before a large view window in the northwest corner of the living room in my home, some sixty feet above and one hundred fifty feet east of the Pacific, where countless times during the forty years I have

Artist's depiction of *yellow* tentacles that slithered from the Pacific in front of author's home at Depoe Bay, an estimated fourteen feet. (Sketch by Judy Limbaugh)

lived here I have thrilled at the sight of seals and sea lions capering and playing in the ocean breakers and occasionally whales rolling along the rocky shore appearing to scrape their sides against the rocks.

Nothing in my experience remotely approached the awesome sight of these writhing *yellow* tentacles appearing like rubber hose, about fourteen feet in visible length and thick as a man's thigh where they disappeared from view in the turgid depths.

I remembered having read about an octopus floating dead being spotted from the bridge of a freighter plodding across the Indian Ocean. It was so huge they changed course to heave to alongside, hoisted it aboard with the ship's cargo crane and measured it. It turned out to be the largest octopus in recorded history at an astounding one hundred ten feet between stretched-out tentacles.

Immobilized with terror, I stood watching for a giant body to come slithering on to the rocks and start eating homes and people.

Then one by one the tentacles started withdrawing into the depths and finally disappeared.

For some time I stood gaping at the spot but it never appeared again.

As it headed west across the bottom of the Pacific its ponderous body created six-foot whirlpools on the surface.

No one else reported seeing the creature, and it was four years before I summoned the courage to tell anyone about what I'd seen, in the thought that I'd be ridiculed out of the county.

16. Sea Transformation

After ripping the sea unabated through most of July, the demented wind at last subsided sometime during the night in early August. When I awoke the quiet was so complete it was almost eerie.

I rolled from my bunk and peered through the wheelhouse windows at a star studded sky swept clear of fog. The stars in the sky's eastern quadrant were beginning to pale, and some high cirrus clouds glowed pink, then burst into flame as the dazzling edge of the sun cracked the Coast Range rim.

The storm gods had vented their wrath and withdrawn. Fair weather and calm seas blessed the Lincoln County coast through nearly all of August.

Like the first stirrings of animals following long hibernation the harbor came to life. The fleet became a bustle of skippers and crewmen shipshaping and readying their gear and warming up engines. Commercial fishing and charter vessels thrashed to sea in continuous procession, us among them.

The sea lay calm as a gently waving sheet of silk, reflecting the sky in the living blue of a kingfisher's wing feathers. The sea, too, came to life in a fantastic air — sea show of nature's creatures.

The prolonged wind had churned nutrients from the bottom of the sea to its surface in upwellings, spurring wild feeding frenzies. Sea birds of all types had gone crazy, thousands upon thousands of them squawking, whirling and diving helter-skelter over and into the ocean·as far as the eye could see.

The wind veered to easterly carrying a strong fragrance

Acres of Albatross and other sea birds (From author's collection)

of cedar and other Coast Range vegetation many miles offshore.

Myriads of multi-colored butterflies were carried over the sea, along with deer flies and other insects. Great numbers of wild canaries were borne on the wind, including one obviously lost and exhausted that circled our vessel several times, then landed on the edge of the binnacle, where with clawed feet gripping the binnacle edge it stood swaying to the pitch and roll of the vessel while it stared at the compass.

Finally after several minutes, it appeared to get squared away on its bearings, took off and flew unerringly east toward land.

Here and there the sea's surface was pocked with the heads of sleek hair seals and ton-sized stellar sea lions bursting from the blue surface with salmon clamped crosswise in their mouths. They played with their catches like a cat with a mouse, tossing the gleaming silver salmon in the air time after time and unerringly catching them in their mouths and shaking their heads furiously, then repeating the process until they tired of their play.

Then they would swallow their prey in a few head-thrusting gulps, bark a couple of times, and dive for more victims.

The triangular dorsal fins of sharks slashed the sea's gently heaving surface in many sectors as the swift, vicious predators competed with other creatures in the berserk feeding fracas. Salmon hit the angler's lines and were boated fast and furiously, as though the fish were eager to escape the rampaging enemies in their watery domain.

"Thar she blows!"

The angler's shouts cut through the bedlam in high pitched excitement. Close on our port beam a pair of whales, rolling in graceful unison, heaved their boxcar-sized backs from the sea, geysered their warm stinking snout spray across our decks, arched their backs and submerged in a shallow dive.

Five minutes later they again rolled their barnacle-pocked backs from the ocean a short way to the south, spouted, thrust their immense twin-fluked tails high in the air and plummeted from sight in their deep sounding dive. We identified them as humpback whales from the glimpse we got of the huge wing-like flippers they use for steering.

Humpbacks, which grow to a length of around fifty feet, are of the group known as baleen whales because, instead of teeth, as in the toothed-whale group, they are equipped with baleen, a wall of bristly slats that grow from the upper jaw and act as a strainer.

Baleens include the enormous blue whales, the largest living creatures on earth. In March, 1926, a blue whale was taken near the Shetland Islands, off Scotland, that was so huge when it was hauled out on the ways it was measured and proved to be an astounding 109 feet, 4½ inches in length, establishing it as the largest in recorded whaling history. Its an anomaly of nature that these largest of all creatures feed mostly on plankton, one of the sea's tiniest organisms.

August sailed along fair and calm, and with mild weather came a transition in the ocean. It gradually warmed and took on a sapphire-blue hue, clear as a mountain lake.

Old timers opined that the tropical-like water of the Japanese Current had swept inshore from its normal flow, fifty to two hundred miles offshore. The change slowed the salmon runs but brought strange new creatures.

Their arrival was heralded overhead by majestic white albatrosses swooping and soaring on graceful wings reaching up to twelve feet from tip to tip.

Masters of the art of riding air currents for hours on end, with scarcely a flap of their great wings, albatrosses live most of their lives far from land, drinking ocean water and sleeping on the sea's surface. A mysterious nature-endowed sense leads them to areas of the greatest number of fish, squid and other small marine animals they mostly feed on; thus, here they were many miles inshore from their normal habitat.

Along with a few salmon, we started catching large numbers of hake, a skinny dull silver gray fish up to three feet in length. We had learned that American fishermen consider them inedible and a nuisance, so we chucked them overboard.

Many years later, hake — renamed whiting — leaped to prominence as an edible fish and are presently harvested by the thousands of tons.

Pacific mackerel, too, frequently hit our lures. Streamlined and an iridescent metallic blue, it reaches nearly two feet in length and is a tasty food fish. Another edible stranger to us was the slate-black sable fish which grows to over three feet in length and often strikes in schools that hit every hook.

Our most "shocking" catch was a three-foot flat fish, sporting black polka dots on its broad light-gray back. When I grabbed it to remove the hook, it zapped me with a nasty electric shock, and I flung it to the deck.

Later I learned that it was an electric ray, which possesses a large pair of electric organs on each side of the head capable of producing a strong electric charge.

It must be touched at two points to get the full shock, which is strong enough to temporarily paralyze a man's arm or knock him down should he step on one lying partially buried in the sand.

Fishermen venturing farther offshore than normal in quest of salmon reported catching large numbers of a fish they didn't recognize so they threw them back into the sea. These fish turned out to be albacore tuna, now prized as "chicken of the sea", an annual multi-million dollar fishery.

Toughing it out for salmon farther inshore, we were amazed to find ourselves escorted now and then by squadrons of warm-water porpoises — beautiful creatures, jet black on their upper bodies and sheet white underneath.

For several minutes they'd leapfrog alongside and dart back and forth across the bow like kids at play. Then as if at a signal, they'd go skittering off through the waves to look for another plaything.

Occasionally we'd happen onto seals floating sound asleep on their backs in the warm water, flippers folded over their bodies like old men dozing in their easy chairs.

17. Here Come the Russians!

A series of cresting seas crashed over our bow and swept us from stem to stern.

The date was April 19, 1966, and we were slugging westward across Yaquina bar at Newport aboard our charter fishing cruiser heading out onto the Pacific in the attempt to locate the Russian fishing fleet that had been reported operating off the Oregon coast for several days.

Among those aboard was Zane Phoenix, who has a master's degree in the Russian language, had made two trips to Russia and was teaching the Russian language at Springfield, Oregon, high school.

Phoenix was hoping for the chance to converse with the Russians.

After bucking into choppy, wind-whipped seas for nearly three hours, we spotted the top hamper of one of the mother ships operating with the Russian trawler fleet. Her position was about twenty five miles west by south of Yaquina Bay.

She was steaming slowly into six foot northwesterly swells.

In those days glasnost was not being practiced by the Russians, and it was to be several years before Gorbachev was to rise to power with his inception of openness and honesty. We had been brainwashed to think of the Russians as bitter enemies.

We approached the Russian ship with a feeling of great trepidation, half expecting to be staring into the muzzles of Russian guns.

As we got closer we could see that we were indeed staring into muzzles — of Russians cameras. They were

Crewmen stare from Russian mothership 25 miles west of Newport. (Photo by author)

as interested in taking pictures of us as we were in taking photos of them.

We approached to within a few feet of her.

Her decks were crowded with people. Dozens lined her rails, grinning and waving at us as we approached.

Some were playing volleyball on the afterdeck.

They tossed Russian magazines and packs of Russian cigarettes to us, and we sent American magazines and cigarettes up to them, which they pounced on eagerly.

We saw many women, who comprised part of the crew and appeared to be clean, comely and neatly attired.

The ship was not neat.

Its dark grey hull and white superstructure were streaked with rust and grime, attesting to its having been at sea for many months.

A heavy fish odor hung over it attracting swarms of sea gulls.

On each side of the stack were large hammer and sickle emblems emblazoned in red.

The red Russian flag fluttered from its flagstaff astern.

Strings of huge fenders were slung along its sides to cushion the hulls of catcher ships when they came alongside to unload.

Russian lettering on the stern, translated by Phoenix, showed the ship's name to be *First of May*, home port Vladivostok.

"The First of May", Phoenix explained "is Russia's most important holiday".

"What size is your ship?" Phoenix shouted in Russian.

"Three hundred twenty five feet long, 3000 tons," came the ready reply.

"How long have you been away from Russia?"

"Four months."

"What kind of fish are you catching?"

"Big perch."

"How many women do you have aboard?"

"Mnogo," (which means many), was the prompt reply.

Phoenix got no answers to his shouted questions as to how many Russian vessels are operating off the Oregon coast.

The Russians indicated that they planned to remain in the area about another month.

As we got underway headed for port the Russians waved and laughed and wished us smooth sailing, according to Phoenix.

As we churned toward port, we concluded that the common man in Russia is like people the world over, seeking love, happiness and the pleasure of living.

Author shows Russian cigarettes given by Russian crewmen aboard mothership (Photo by Jim Haron)

18. Wreck of the
USS *Milwaukee*

The United States Navy submarine *H-3* battled through heavy breakers on a stormy outbound crossing of Columbia River bar in December, 1916, following a visit to Portland.

The buffeting wrenched battery connections loose, causing partial electrical failure, and disabled one diesel.

Laboring on one engine, the battered sub clawed alongside the Columbia River lightship, where Lt. (jg) Harry Bogusch, commanding officer, braced against the periscope standards on the surfaced sub's bridge, ordered a southerly heading toward Eureka, California, next scheduled port of call.

His order was the first in a series of events that was to end in one of the navy's most disastrous fiascos.

Dawn came sluggishly as the *H-3*, still on one engine, groped southward through long gray Pacific ground swells off the northern California coast December 15.

On the bridge Lt. Bogusch, with his officer of the watch, a quartermaster petty officer, and a seaman lookout, stared through binoculars ahead and inshore for a glimpse of buoys and beacons marking the approach channel leading into Humboldt Bay and Eureka.

A mixture of mist and smoke from coastal lumber mills squeezed visibility down to a few hundred yards.

Abruptly the lookout reported an object on the port beam.

All four stared through their glasses in the direction of the lookout's point and discerned a narrow dark object protruding from the murk.

Assuming it to be a Humboldt Bay entrance marker, Lt. Bogusch ordered the helm put to port for an easterly heading through the channel — he thought.

The sub, which had been rolling heavily while cruising beam-on to the swells, began a series of plunging rushes as she swung to port and began running with the inrushing seas, white water creaming on either side of the conning tower as she leaped ahead on steepening crests.

Suddenly a peaking sea heaved the sub's stern high, then broke in a crashing maelstrom over its entire length, broaching it to starboard.

Backing full on one engine was to no avail. The sub rammed hard aground broadside on the sandy bottom, rolling viciously in pounding breakers.

The four men ducked quickly below, battening the water-tight hatches behind them.

U.S. Navy submarine *H-3* aground at Samoa Beach, near Eureka, California. Sub was later hauled on rollers over wooden tracks across half-mile-wide sandspit, re-launched in Humboldt Bay, repaired at Mare Island Navy Yard, and served in World War I. (From author's collection)

An urgent SOS was sent requesting speed in rescue because several men had been injured and battery gas was filling the sub.

The *H-3* had grounded on Samoa Beach, a long, half-mile-wide sand spit that stretches north from the Humboldt-channel entrance.

The radio operator at the Samoa Beach Lifesaving Station received the call, and the lifesaving crew quickly trundled its cart-transported surfboat from its boathouse and labored with it across three miles of sandy beach, where they found the *H-3* pounding murderously, 300 yards offshore.

On the sandspit a short distance to the east a smoke-stack rearing from the mist at a nearby lumber mill revealed itself as the object, mistaken for a channel marker, that had lured the *H-3* to disaster.

The lifesaving crew deemed the breakers too heavy to risk launching the surfboat, so a Lyle line-throwing cannon was quickly rigged and on the second attempt a line was fired across the sub's breaker-bashed deck.

Shortly, a man clambered from the conning tower, secured the line as high as possible and scrambled below. He had no sooner dropped from sight than the sub rolled to seaward, almost on beams end, and the line parted.

Another line was shot across the sub, but no one came from below to make it fast. Battery gas and the terrible buffeting inside the sub had so stupefied those aboard that no one was capable of climbing up through the lurching conning tower.

Speedy action must be taken if death to all hands was to be averted.

The only alternative was to launch the surfboat. Without hesitation the surfmen shoved the cart into the frothing surf, launched their bucking craft safely and battled through roaring combers to the wallowing sub.

Watching their chances between breakers, lest the boat be shattered against the sub's rolling steel side, the surfmen worked close enough to permit some of their men to leap aboard, where they secured and rigged the hauling line and breeches buoy apparatus.

All 27 of the bruised, groggy officers and men aboard the *H-3* wre hauled safely ashore.

Giant combers during the following high tides drove the *H-3* farther onto the beach until at low tide she lay high and dry on the sand.

Inspection showed her hull to be virtually undamaged. Naval officers at Mare Island Navy Yard, on San Francisco Bay at Vallejo, began laying salvage plans.

They decided that the 1,000-horsepower navy tug *Iroquois,* towing in tandem with the 2,400-horsepower navy tender *Cheyenne,* should be able to tow the stranded sub from the beach into deep water. The Cheyenne and the Coast Guard cutter *McCullough* had been standing by off Samoa Beach since shortly after the *H-3's* stranding to assist in salvage operations.

Steaming from Mare Island, the *Iroquois* arrived off Samoa Beach and anchored just outside the first line of breakers, some 500 yards offshore. Radio communication was immediately established with the *H-3's* crew, who had pitched camp on the sand spit near their stranded vessel and were standing by with a 10-inch hawser to be used in the towing attempt.

Getting the line through the surf to the salvage vessels presented a nasty problem. First a light line must be run from the *Iroquois* to shore. Then heavier lines would be attached successively until a line stout enough to haul the heavy towing hawser to the tug could be run.

The surf was considered too heavy to risk lives by launching a boat from one of the salvage vessels and running the line through the breakers to the beach with it.

Repeated attempts to float lines attached to buoys, life rafts and empty ship's boats through the breakers to shore failed. The weight of the line attached to them created too much drag.

Finally, in desperation, Lt. Bogusch, the sub's skipper, who had rowed on varsity crews at the Naval Academy, borrowed a surfboat from the lifesaving station, rounded up a volunteer crew and pulling stroke oar himself, battled through the breakers to the *Cheyenne* with a "messenger" line, and by bending on successively heavier lines the towing hawser was finally hauled to the *Cheyenne* and secured.

On the next high tide, the *Cheyenne* and *Iroquois*, towing in tandem with the *Iroquois* in the lead, took a strain. Slowly the big hawser rose dripping from the sea, then stretched taut.

The *H-3's* bow swiveled a few feet toward the sea, then brought up solidly, stuck fast in the sand, stopping the straining towing vessels dead.

Using every ounce of their combined 3,400 horsepower, their propellers beating the sea's surface into a frothing maelstrom, they could not budge the sub. Finally the big hawser parted.

The month's highest tides had now passed, storm warnings had been broadcast and the sea was building, forcing suspension of salvage efforts. Treacherous breakers on Humboldt bar prevented entry into the harbor at Eureka; so the salvage vessels steamed to San Francisco Bay to await further developments.

The Mare Island Navy Yard commandant, who was in charge of salvage operations, decided to offer the *H-3* salvage job to civilian firms and called for bids.

Two bids were received. One was submitted by one of the most experienced salvage firms on the west coast. For $150,000 it proposed to winch the sub off the beach into deep water with heavy steel cables secured to winches on the deck of a fully-equipped salvage vessel securely anchored outside the breaker line.

The second bid was submitted by the Fraser Lumber Company, of Eureka, which offered to do the job for a surprisingly-low $18,000. They proposed to accomplish it by constructing a double-track timber runway across the sandspit to Humboldt Bay, jacking the sub onto rollers and hauling it over the track for re-launching in the quiet waters of the bay.

Navy officers turned down the first bid as being too expensive and all but scoffed at the second bid, which they rejected on the grounds that it was too small an amount to accomplish the job.

Officers decided the navy could pull the *H-3* free by using a more powerful ship, assisted by the *Iroquois* and *Cheyenne.*

The 10,000-ton, 24,000-horsepower cruiser *Milwaukee,*

valued at $7,000,000 and manned by nearly 450 officers and men, was decided upon to do the job.

Accompanied by the *Iroquois* and *Cheyenne*, the mighty *Milwaukee* steamed through the Golden Gate and up the coast to Samoa Beach, where she dropped anchor seaward of the *H-3*, some four ship's lengths outside the outermost breaker line.

Crewmen at Camp H-3 radioed the *Milwaukee* that the sub had been driven farther up on the beach during the last storm but had suffered little damage. They added that the surf was too heavy to risk pulling through it in a surfboat to the *Milwaukee* with a line.

The job would have to be done from the ships. Remembering all too well their frustrating earlier attempts to float a line ashore from the *Iroquois*, navymen had this time come prepared — they thought.

The *Iroquois* had towed to the site a steel barge equipped with steel fins which had been welded to its sides at Mare Island. The fins, it was thought, would catch the force of the inrushing swells and heave the barge into the surf and onto the beach with its all-important line.

Failure again. The barge drifted to within a few yards of the first breaker line, where it lay pitching and rolling, refusing to go another inch.

Time was growing short. A new winter storm could strike at any time, and a threatening black wall of fog was hanging over the sea along the horizon in the west.

Aboard the *Milwaukee* the officer in charge of salvage operations decided that a crew would have to run the line ashore with a pulling boat.

Those aboard the *Milwaukee* who had had surf experience shook their heads, aware that waves whose back sides look deceptively serene become crashing killers on their breaking frontal sides.

The salvage officer's decision stood. In response to the *Milwaukee* captain's signalled request for the loan of a sea-worthy pulling boat, a crew from the Coast Guard cutter *McCullough*, anchored nearby, pulled smartly alongside in a surf boat.

The Coast Guard crew boarded the *Milwaukee* and was replaced by a navy crew, consisting of an officer, a coxswain, eight oarsmen and a man to play out the line being run to the beach.

Pulling strongly, they headed toward the surf through huge swells that blocked out all sight of both land and ships when they dropped into the yawning troughs.

Certain disaster was portended by the burly, sea-wise Coast Guard warrant officer who had been in charge of the surf-boat when it was brought from the *McCullough*.

He was right.

As it reached the breaker line the hapless surfboat was caught in a murderous rush of giant combers that hurled it cartwheeling end over end, spewing men and oars in all directions.

Watchers ashore stared horrified as the surfboat and its occupants were catapulted through the air. They fanned out along the beach to watch for survivors, and each time a foundering man was spotted — some unconscious, some injured, some delirious — human chains were formed to snatch them to safety.

Those needing medical aid were rushed to the nearby Hammond Lumber Company infirmary for treatment.

Miraculously, only one man was lost. His body was found the next day some distance to the south near the Humboldt harbor entrance.

The capsized surfboat, meantime, had drifted in close enough for the watching men to haul it onto the beach. The line to the *Milwaukee* was still attached. The mission had been accomplished — at a steep price.

Starting with the line carried in by the surfboat, successively larger lines were run to the *Milwaukee,* and at long last a five-inch and a six-inch steel cable were run and secured to a towing shackle in the *H-3's* stem.

On the *Milwaukee* a 15-fathom length of 2½-inch chain was secured to the end of each towing cable. The chains were run through the *Milwaukee's* port and starboard quarter chocks, then shackled to heavy steel cables that had been wound around a steel after deckhouse to provide sturdy towing purchase.

Strangely, pelican hooks, which would have made it possible to release the towing cables quickly in case of emergency, were not used. This omission was to spell disaster.

On the next high tide the first attempt to free the sub was made. Shouldering her 24,000 horses of steam power into the job, the *Milwaukee* pulled mightily, clouds of black smoke swirling from her four stacks, huge scallops of white water cataracting from her counter.

The *H-3* ground through the sand a few feet, then stopped. The powerful *Milwaukee* could not budge her another inch, and the *Milwaukee's* captain decided to wait until a higher tide crested at 3 a.m. the following day; then again tackle the tow.

Hearing this via the radio at Camp H-3, the officer in charge of Samoa Beach Lifesaving Station, wise in the ways of sea and weather on this stretch of coast, offered Lt. Bogusch some straightforward advice.

He pointed out that the sea was rising, a strong southerly set of current had built up along the coast, a fog bank hanging offshore was almost a cinch to move in during the night and warned that if the *Milwaukee* were to hoist her anchor and try to tow in fog and darkness, she'd almost certainly be carried south by the current and be in grave danger of going aground herself.

Lt. Bogusch communicated this advice to the *Milwaukee's* skipper, but he was not to be dissuaded, pointing out that the *Iroquois* would have a line on the *Milwaukee's* starboard bow and could exert enough pull to offset the current. Moreover, he argued, the *Cheyenne* would be standing by and if necessary could take a line from the *Milwaukee's* bow and haul directly seaward, thus adding her 2,400 horsepower to the pull.

He won his point — unfortunately.

As the lifesaving skipper had predicted, the sea built, the southerly set increased and the fog rolled in. The *Milwaukee's* captain ignored nature's warnings and shortly before 3 a.m. ordered the anchor hoisted, and the tow attempt began. But not for long.

With the anchor up, the great cruiser began swinging in an arc to the south, slowly, inexorably; closer and closer to the thundering breakers; trapped by the taut towing cables attached to the beached *H-3*, 3,000 feet astern.

Both bower anchors were dropped, but at short stay they did little to hold the cruiser against the powerful current and steepening seas.

The urgent order was shouted to let go the towing lines — on the double!

The *Milwaukee's* huskiest sailors frantically swung heavy sledge hammers at the shackle pins. The strain was too great. The sailors' pounding blows succeeded only in driving the pins from the eyes on one side of the shackles; then they jammed.

Other sailors attacked the cables with hacksaws, sawing feverishly but futilely.

A searchlight on the *Milwaukee's* foremast stabbed into foggy darkness in search of the *Cheyenne.* A towline from her was needed desperately. The *Cheyenne* could not be found.

The searchlight swung to starboard, following the taut towing hawser to the straining *Iroquois.* The tug was fighting a losing battle. The *Milwaukee* was dragging her relentlessly stern-ward toward the breakers. Sailors on the *Iroquois* stood by the hawser with axes.

The wallowing *Milwaukee* was trapped.

She rose beam-on over a curling sea, then struck bottom in the following trough with a sledgehammer shudder. The next sea lifted her briefly, then slammed her onto the bottom again . . . and again . . . and again, broadside in the breakers.

Towering combers crashed over her seaward side, driving her farther and farther inshore. Her bottom was stove in, decks buckled, boilers shifted, steam lines broken, fires extinguished.

Engine room personnel were forced to flee topside. All hands rushed for upper decks, donning life jackets as they scrambled up tilting ladders and across lurching decks. They clung for dear life to whatever they could on the leeward side, away from the murderous breakers.

Incredibly the big cruiser, which had a 22-foot draft, was driven inshore to a scant 12-foot depth, where she lay pounding with a 20 degree starboard list.

At the first terrifying thump on the ocean floor, the *Milwaukee's* skipper had radioed the *Iroquois* and *Cheyenne* to keep clear, hold to deep water; the *Milwaukee* was beyond help.

Towering breaker crashing over *USS Milwaukee's* starboard side. (Note steam still billowing from stacks before boilers flooded.) (From author's collection)

Axe-wielding sailors on the *Iroquois* hacked furiously at the towing hawser and soon severed it. The tug slammed sea-ward to safety.

The *Milwaukee's* terse radio message was picked up by the Table Bluff Radio Station, 4½ miles south of the Humboldt Bay channel entrance, which quickly relayed it to the Samoa Beach Lifesaving Station.

Lifesaving crewmen again went into quick action and shortly fired a line from their Lyle cannon into the foggy darkness in what they fervently hoped was the right range and direction.

The first shot missed but a following shot thumped the line-carrying projectile onto the cruiser's deck. Sailors quickly secured it and hauled aboard and rigged the breeches buoy apparatus.

The thunderous roar of the breakers, as the lifesaving crew rushed its rescue work, was punctuated by eerie shrieks of the Hammond Lumber Mill's steam whistle, which by prearrangement screeched the news that the *Milwaukee* was aground.

Hundreds of the local citizenry rushed to Samoa Beach, where they built huge bonfires, prepared hot coffee, and

U.S. Navy cruiser *Milwaukee* aground at Samoa Beach near Eureka, California. The ship, valued at $7,000,000, was a total loss. (From author's collection)

10,000-ton U.S. Navy cruiser *Milwaukee* aground at Samoa Beach near Eureka, California. (From author's collection)

stood ready with blankets and booze to warm the shipwrecked sailors.

By the time several men had been hauled ashore in the breeches buoy, the receding tide had left the *Milwaukee* lying nearly stationary on the sandy bottom, about 300 yards from shore. Approaching in the lee created by the wrecked cruiser, rescuers were able to bring the remaining crewmen ashore in surfboats without loss of life.

At the navy's tragically belated request, the Fraser Lumber Company, still standing by its $18,000 bid, put its men to work. In a comparatively short time they laid redwood tracks across the spit's half-mile width, jacked the sub onto rollers, hauled it to Humboldt Bay and re-launched it.

The *Iroquois* towed the *H-3* to Mare Island Navy yard, where it was reconditioned and later sailed away to fight in World War I.

Through the years the once-proud USS *Milwaukee* has succumbed to the ravages of the sea and wreckers' torches, and today nothing remains but a few rusted chunks of metal, a dismal reminder of the navy's calamitous goof.

19. Capsizing of the Steam Schooner *Brooklyn*

The deep-throated blast of the steam schooner *Brooklyn's* steam whistle reverberated across the wind-chopped waters of Humboldt Bay at Eureka, California, as the ship cast off from the "E" Street wharf and headed for the distant bar, which she planned to cross en route to sea.

No one could know that the shriek of the whistle preluded doom. This was the start of the ship's last voyage.

The ominous roar of thunderous breakers on Humboldt bar warned of dangerously heavy seas.

On the bridge that late afternoon of November 8, 1930, Captain J.T. Tufvesson of Berkeley stared ahead through the approaching murky dusk. Keeping watch alongside of him was his chief officer, Jorgen Grieve of San Francisco.

Following the *Brooklyn* a few hundred yards astern was another steam schooner, the *Washington,* commanded by Captain Julius G. Ahlin.

As the two steamers ventured toward the bar on ebb tide, the fury of the breakers pounding over shoals became apparent.

Captain Ahlin saw the *Brooklyn* lose headway as she reached the maelstrom of pounding seas, and decided to turn back to port while he could.

The *Brooklyn* was just clearing the breakwater when two towering breakers slugged her in the bow, one after another, smashing in the hatches, permitting tons of sea water to pour into the engine room, putting out the boiler fires and causing her to lose power.

John Ferrazo, lookout at North Jetty, heard four blasts on the *Brooklyn's* whistle, indicating distress and called the Coast Guard Station in the bay.

Steam schooner *Brooklyn* capsized on Humboldt Bar Eureka, California, while attempting to cross to sea across rough bar. First mate, found clinging to wreckage three days later, was sole survivor. (From author's collection)

She sheared off to the north and seas broke over her repeatedly, driving her on to her starboard beam. Crewmen clawed their way up the steeply sloping deck until finally she capsized and sank.

Immediately Captain Gunnar Churchill and crew put out from the Coast Guard station with the power boat. They patrolled the sea off the entrance throughout the night but could find no trace of any survivors. The tug *Humboldt* also dashed to the scene but due to the high seas could not get out over the bar.

The next morning thousands of persons searched the beach from the north jetty to a point a mile or so north of the wreck of the USS *Milwaukee*. The beach was covered with debris — shattered sections of lifeboats, broken oars, pieces from the deck and saloon structure, water soaked ship's stores, life preservers and countless other items of flotsam.

On the morning of November 11, the fishing vessel *Two Sisters*, Captain Dick Richter, left Humboldt Bay on a fishing trip. The seas were littered with wreckage of the

Brooklyn for several miles out. While they were looking at the wreckage, Richter suddenly sighted something that looked like a man hanging on to a bit of the debris.

As the *Two Sisters* neared the wreckage, the object became plainer, and it soon became evident that it was a man, most of his clothes torn off. It was Jorgen Grieve, First Officer of the *Brooklyn,* who had been floating with the wreckage for 72 hours in the open sea.

Prying loose his grip, they gently lifted him aboard and took him into the cabin where a blanket replaced what little clothing remained. After pouring hot coffee down his throat, they gave him a seaman's trousers and coat, and let him fall into a deep sleep.

The *Two Sisters* immediately headed at top speed for Eureka. At the foot of "F" Street Grieve was placed in an ambulance and rushed toward the old St. Joseph's Hospital at Trinity and "F" Streets. But the man who was snatched from death at sea was to face death from another avenue before he reached the hospital bed! At Wabash and "F" Streets the ambulance collided with an automobile and was damaged to such an extent that it could go no further. Attendants carried Grieve on a stretcher the remaining five blocks to the hospital.

In spite of his exhausted condition from clinging to a bit of wreckage for three days without food or water, Dr. Chain said he would live. When Grieve regained consciousness, he asked after his fellow sailors.

Following Grieve's dramatic rescue, bodies of the Brooklyn's crew were found as they washed ashore along with huge amounts of flotsam and wreckage.

Inspectors Frank Turner and Joseph Dolan, from San Francisco, interviewed witnesses and examined the wreckage. They said the *Brooklyn* was in first class condition despite her twenty eight years, and not a piece of rotten timber from her was found.

On the eighteenth, after recovering sufficiently to travel, Grieve returned to San Francisco. At the Ferry Building he was greeted by his wife and daughter amid cheering crowds before he was driven to the U.S. Marine Hospital for further recuperation.

When the steam schooner *Washington* arrived in San

Francisco Captain Julius G. Ahlin took the witness stand as Steamboat Inspection hearings were concluded. He told of following the *Brooklyn* about 800 feet astern of her, seeing her in trouble and ordering his own vessel put about just in time to avoid a similar fate. He declared his belief that Captain Tufvesson should never have ventured passage on the bar on an ebb tide.

The verdict told how the vessel was knocked broadside to the waves and could not head into them because the sea washed into the boiler room putting out the fires. Captain Turner said that in his opinion if the *Brooklyn,* which was running with a very small cargo, had been carrying her usual deck load of lumber, she would not have capsized and sunk.

Turner and Dolan's verdict declared Captain Tufvesson a good steam schooner man, and they did not find him at fault.

Offsetting the tragedy of the loss of the *Brooklyn* and her men, one inspiring event stood out; Jorgen Grieve's ability to hang on until rescued and return safely to his family.

20. Destroyer Disaster

With foaming white bones in their teeth and curling rooster tails astern the fourteen sleek grey destroyers of Destroyer Squadron Eleven churned past the Columbia River mouth cruising from the Washington coast, where they had been undergoing a summer of fleet maneuvers, headed for their home port of San Diego after a stop at San Francisco.

The destroyermen's high spirits at the prospect of returning to home port would have been shattered on that early September day in 1923 had they known that they were to be hurled to destruction in a few days in the worst peace-time disaster in the history of the U.S. Navy.

The voyage to San Francisco was uneventful, and after several days of rest and relaxation in the bay city the squadron steamed through the Golden Gate and then to San Francisco Lightship where course 160° was set at the start of the final leg of the voyage to San Diego.

The destroyers had been constructed during World War I and were the best designed in the U.S. Navy. They were 314 feet long and had a beam of 32 feet, a displacement of 1,250 tons and a draft of nearly 10 feet.

Each destroyer had two 27,000 horsepower steam engines which gave them a top speed of 32 knots with their twin propellers. Normally each destroyer carried a crew of 114, but due to post-war budget problems carried a crew 20 to 30 per cent smaller.

The Commodore in command of Squadron Eleven, Captain Edward H. Watson, had been given orders by the commanding officer of the destroyer squadrons, Admiral E.W. Kitelle, to maintain a full twenty-knot speed as an engineering test for the San Francisco to San Diego trip of about 430 miles.

Captain Watson was a highly respected Naval Academy graduate who had served as Captain of the Battleship *Alabama* during the first World War. Assignments as U.S. Naval Attache at the American Embassy in Tokyo were among other interesting duties.

Because of the endurance drill conditions given to them, Squadron Eleven left after the bulk of the fleet. Watson, in his lead flagship the *Delphy,* led the fourteen-ship squadron in three columns. Each ship in the column was to maintain a distance of only 150 yards between the stern of the preceding ship and its own bow.

With darkness a light fog set in along the coast. The destroyers continued to maintain their 20-knot speed. As the ships neared the Santa Barbara Channel, the fog became more dense. The signal "Form 18" was hoisted by *Delphy,* and in compliance the other ships formed a single column astern of her.

Each destroyer had a navigator, but the orders of the Chief Navigator on the *Delphy* were to be followed by all ships. Their orders were to follow the lead of the *Delphy* and stay in close formation in the column. Radar was not available to ships in 1923. Some radio navigation facilities had been recently installed, but naval officers had little faith in them or the new radio directional finding stations (RDF) on shore.

Captain Watson, LCDR Donald T. Hunter, commanding officer of the *Delphy,* and LT (JG) Blodgett, technically the navigational officer on the *Delphy,* plotted their course by dead reckoning. A radio direction finding station was located on Point Arguello and was in operation as Squadron Eleven neared the Santa Barbara Channel in the evening. The Squadron had been on a south compass course.

At 8:30 in the evening, the officers on the *Delphy* planned to turn east after passing south and clearing Point Arguello. The dead reckoning position the officers plotted on their charts indicated that the *Delphy* was south of Point Arguello and about 12 miles out to sea. The *Delphy* commanding officer mistakenly thought that if the Squadron continued any longer on their southerly course, they would run aground on San Miguel Island.

The *Delphy* took a radio bearing from the Point Arguello RDF Station. The bearing indicated that the *Delphy* was still north and just offshore of Point Arguello. The bearing was determined later to be accurate. Watson and Hunter, however, did not believe the radio station's bearing, trusting their dead reckoning position and calculation.

Some confusion occurred on the bridge during this period as signals were being received from the Pacific Mail freighter *Cuba* which had run aground on San Miguel Island. The *Cuba* was sending SOS signals and rescue ships were in close radio contact with her, cluttering up the radio airwaves. The commingling of distress signals caused some confusion to the navigators.

Another radio bearing was received from Point Arguello Station which still placed the squadron north of Arguello and closer to shore than their plotted position indicated. Blodgett, who believed in the radio direction system, said to his two senior officers, "the bearings have been erratic by a few degrees, captain, but they have all put us north of the Point. How about slowing for a sounding, sir?".

Commodore Watson and Captain Hunter exchanged glances and Watson said, "no, not much use — probably can't reach bottom — spoil our engineering run."

For lack of faith in a new radio navigational aid, not wanting to spoil a formation pattern, and not respecting the forces in the Channel, the men of Destroyer Squadron Eleven were about to face disaster.

Convinced that the destroyers had passed south of Point Arguello, Watson and Hunter ordered their course changed a few minutes before 9 p.m. to an easterly course of 95°, the normal compass course that would take them through the Santa Barbara Channel. As they changed course, the fog thickened considerably. The captain continued to hold a speed of 20 knots.

Without any warning, the *Delphy* being the lead ship, struck the shore first at full cruising speed. It was 9:05 p.m., September 8, 1923. The ship scraped the bottom gently and then hit the rocks with a head-on crash, smashing to an immediate stop. The *Delphy* crew were hurled about the ship in terrible confusion.

Captain Watson, still not realizing his true position, thought he had hit San Miguel Island 23 miles to the west. He quickly sent a message to the other ships, attempting to warn them away from the rocks. Unfortunately, he radioed the ships to keep clear to westward, make 90°. He only made matters worse. He ordered them to turn more directly into shore.

The *Delphy* had hit the mainland at an area known as Honda, a few miles north of Point Arguello. Seeing that the *Delphy* was sinking Hunter ordered the ship abandoned. The other destroyers, only 150 or so yards behind each other, had little time to change course or stop. Many of them frantically put their engines in reverse but not in time.

The destroyer *S.P. Lee,* astern of the *Delphy* put its engines full astern but had slowed only to 8 knots before slamming into the rocks next to the *Delphy.*

At about two minute intervals, the *Nicholas, Woodbury, Young, Chauncey,* and *Fuller,* following trustingly astern of their commodore, sickeningly crashed into the vicious, rocky coastline. The fog was so thick along the shore the ships could not see each other.

Fortunately, the other destroyers in the squadron listening to the calls and warnings and being a little suspicious of the dead reckoning of the lead ship, had slowed, pulled back, and gone into reverse in time. Even with their quick thinking, two of them touched bottom and one was damaged slightly in maneuvering out of the rough seas and rocky surroundings.

The grounded ships pounded and twisted in crazy confusion on the rocks and pounding waves. The *Young* turned over, trapping 20 men below. The officers and men aboard all the ships responded quickly and efficiently to the horror they now faced.

Because the rear echelon destroyer commanders did hold back and did not steer a 90° course into the rocks, as ordered, they saved their ships. However, the captains who did follow orders, saw their destroyers become wrecked additions to Arguello's graveyard of ships.

A Southern Pacific Railroad foreman, John Giorvas,

who lived nearby in a company house had looked out his bedroom window before going to bed and had seen flashes of light. Opening his bedroom window, he listened, heard noises and went down the mesa to the coast to investigate.

Almost in disbelief, he witnessed the destroyers grinding and twisting in agony in the sea.

Giorvas quickly called to nearby railroad workers on the plateau above Honda, who rushed to the shore to help the crewmen.

The foreman quickly sent messages out and rescue parties were on their way. Help, including a doctor, came from Lompoc, a small community to the northeast of the area. Rescuers also came from Santa Barbara and from nearby ranches, including a woman by the name of "Ma" Atkins, the wife of a Southern Pacific telegrapher at Surf, five miles north of Honda, who was hoisted to heroine status by working tirelessly making hot coffee, soup and sandwiches, and administering to the needs of the injured.

A total of 800 officers and men were aboard the seven ships. During the night, about 450 of the men got ashore, many with serious injuries. The nearby railroad was used to transport survivors to Santa Barbara and San Luis Obisbo hospitals.

Several fishermen, discovering the disaster, used their boats, courageously maneuvering in and out of the rough seas to rescue the crews.

The fishermen, after rescuing the men, calmly went back to fishing without giving their names to any of the people they rescued.

First aid, blankets and food were rushed to the scene. By the next day, the remaining officers and men made it to shore or were taken aboard rescuing ships. In a roll call, it was determined that 23 men were dead or missing in the disaster, and scores were injured.

The Navy estimated that the loss of the seven destroyers totalled around $13,500,000. In the attempted salvage work, no bodies were found in the wreckage of the destroyers. Ultimately a total of 17 bodies were recovered. The bodies of six men were never found.

The Navy did recover about 80 torpedoes valued at around $5,000 each, guns, and other equipment.

Seven destroyers on rocks at Honda Point, California, were total losses. (From author's collection)

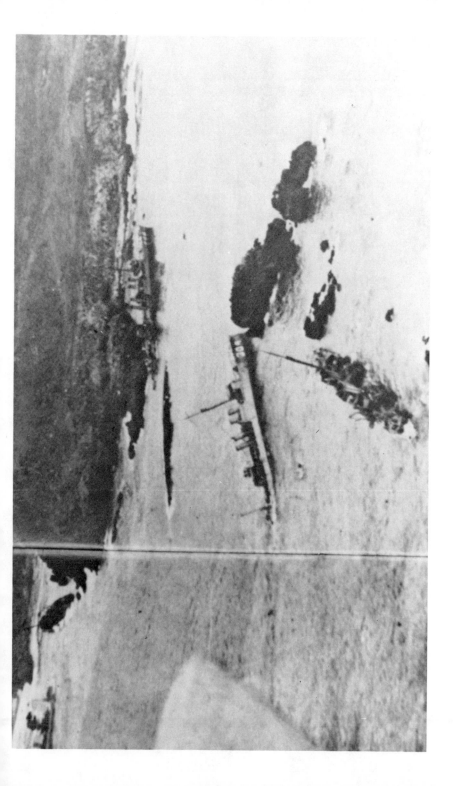

A court martial was ordered for eleven officers, including Watson and Hunter. Charges of culpable inefficiency in the performance of duty were made against the officers. Although ordered to follow their lead ship, some of the squadron skippers were charged with being derelict in their duties for not questioning the navigator's instructions from the *Delphy*.

Many of the officers felt they were "damned if they did and dammed if they didn't". It was made clear to them from the start of the voyage that they were not to interfere with the radio navigational communication of the *Delphy* or to break out of their close formation.

Captain Edward Watson and LCDR Donald Hunter were found guilty of culpable inefficiency and negligence. The other destroyer commanders were found not guilty of negligence as charged, but the Navy Judge Advocate General and Secretary of the Navy, in reviewing the verdicts disapproved of their "not guilty" verdicts. This left a cloud over their future advancement and promotional opportunities in the Navy.

Watson was given a reduction of 150 numbers on the promotional list and Hunter a loss of 100 numbers on the list. They would never be promoted again.

Author in shrouds on *Kingfisher* (Photo by Terry Turner)

ABOUT THE AUTHOR

Stan Allyn lives in a ship-shape home right on the Pacific Ocean, two blocks south of the Depoe Bay Channel entrance, which he first entered in May, 1938, at the tiny seaport town of Depoe Bay, Oregon.

With a converted twenty-eight foot Columbia River gillnetter named *Tradewinds*, equipped with a two-cylinder, eight-horsepower engine, he started the charter fishing business that he still owns.

His son, Richard, directs the operation of the fifteen vessels in the Tradewinds Ocean Sport Fishing fleet and his daughter-in-law Valerie is office manager.

Stan still owns the company but spends most of his time writing about the sea.

His first book, *Heave To! You'll Drown Yourselves!*, is in its third printing.